VIGILANTE ANGELS

Book I: The Priest

Billy DeCarlo

Wild Lake Press, Inc.

Wilmington, DE

Billy DeCarlo/Wild Lake Press, Inc
P.O. Box 7045, Hackettstown, NJ 07840
billydecarlo.com **(blog, newsletter signup)**

Publisher's Note: This is a work of fiction. Names, characters, places, and incidents are a product of the author's imagination. Locales and public names are sometimes used for atmospheric purposes. Any resemblance to actual people, living or dead, or to businesses, companies, events, institutions, or locales is completely coincidental.

Cover by Archangel Ink http://archangelink.com/
Editing by WordVagabond https://wordvagabond.com/

Vigilante Angels Book I: The Priest/ Billy DeCarlo. -- 1st ed.
ISBN 978-0-9972196-4-7
LCCN: 2017943533

Sign up for the newsletter at billydecarlo.com **to stay informed about progress and release dates for new books, audiobooks, and other news.**

Previews of upcoming works and short stories by Billy DeCarlo at Patreon.com/billydecarlo**.**

Other books by Billy DeCarlo:
https://www.billydecarlo.com/index.php/books

To all who have suffered.

"Whoever receives one such child in my name receives me, but whoever causes one of these little ones who believe in me to sin, it would be better for him to have a great millstone fastened around his neck and to be drowned in the depth of the sea. Woe to the world for temptations to sin! For it is necessary that temptations come, but woe to the one by whom the temptation comes! And if your hand or your foot causes you to sin, cut it off and throw it away. It is better for you to enter life crippled or lame than with two hands or two feet to be thrown into the eternal fire. And if your eye causes you to sin, tear it out and throw it away. It is better for you to enter life with one eye than with two eyes to be thrown into the hell of fire. See that you do not despise one of these little ones. For I tell you that in heaven their angels always see the face of my Father who is in heaven."

— MATTHEW 18:5-10

Contents

1 THE PRIEST

THE PRIEST SWEPT ACROSS THE DAIS with grace, although his heart held malice.

A boy watched from a pew near the front of the otherwise empty church. He pretended to flip through a hymnal and contemplated whether his parents would believe him if he decided to run. He imagined his mother at home preparing dinner, proud that the priest had picked him out of all the other altar boys to perform these extra duties after school. Peering over the book, he wondered how the man could move so silently, almost appearing to float. *Are there even legs under those long robes?* He edged closer to the aisle.

"Going somewhere, my son?"

It sounded like the true voice of God. Its deep timbre echoed from the high ceiling and marble walls, surrounding him.

"No, Father." He thought his voice sounded meek by comparison—squeaky and scared. He *was* scared. He tried again, this time in a stronger voice, the more confident one Dad had been coaching him to use. "No." This time it sounded better, at least to him. *Where are you, Dad?*

He looked at the stained-glass figures in the windows above. Their eyes seemed cast down at him in pity. Jesus. Mary. Joseph. He asked for their help. Didn't they stand for goodness? He thought about the superheroes in his comic books and imagined one sailing through the glass to save him. He wondered whether God was looking down, too. *Why doesn't He do anything?*

He watched the priest clean up around the altar. His tall, thin build and long limbs made him look like a praying mantis. The boy's gaze moved upward, to the massive crucifix on the wall above the priest—Jesus pinned to it with his crown of thorns, eyes closed, blood dripping from wounds on his hands, feet, and abdomen.

Fall. Fall on him. Fall on him, Jesus. You're supposed to be the Savior.

A booming sound startled him as the side door slammed behind Charles, the old black maintenance man. The kids all talked about how Charles had done time in prison. Who knew if it was true? That was the least of his worries right now, anyway.

"What else can I do tonight, Father?" Charles asked. He looked over toward the boy.

The boy read a look of concern on his face and tried to respond in kind, staring back hopefully. He trusted Charles, who'd only been nice to him in the time they had spent together, and he'd always felt sorry for the priest's harsh treatment of the man.

"Nothing more, Charles," said the God-voice. "That will be all for today."

Charles began to leave but hesitated. "You sure you don't want me to sweep up in here?"

"That will be all, Charles." The priest was polishing a silver chalice, his back to them both.

Charles looked over at the boy again. "Can I walk the kid home, then? He done here too?"

The priest turned to face them. His ruddy face and red hair seemed to glow under the lights. This time he spoke softly, but his voice commanded an end to the discussion. "That will be all, Charles."

"All right then. See you tomorrow, Father." He walked up the aisle, patting the boy's shoulder on the way past, his footsteps echoing. The thick front door creaked as he opened it.

The boy turned to see Charles pause in the doorway as if pondering some other course of action. Their eyes engaged once more, and hope again filled his heart. Charles held the door wide open for a moment, then lowered his head and left. The boy wondered if he could make it before the door locked behind the janitor. He imagined the priest gliding down the aisle at warp speed on those long legs and grabbing him by the collar just as he reached it. It gasped slowly to closure and shut with a soft, final click. The boy turned to face the dais again but found the priest's robes in his face. There was a swish of satin as a long arm swept up and took hold of his shoulder.

"Come along, son. We have work to do in the rectory before you leave."

The boy rose obediently, and as was his custom, the priest placed his hand on the nape of his neck to guide him, his thumb digging into the gap between vertebrae. *His hands are always so cold.* As they walked by the dais, he gazed at the rows of flickering candles in small red jars, lit for the prayers of others.

2 CHEMO

'm dying. Tommy leaned back in the padded recliner, and the paper on the headrest crinkled. He worried for a moment that the nurses hadn't changed it after the last patient, and then realized the absurdity of his concern. *Anyway, I'm almost bald now.*

The glass faceplate of the infusion console reflected his grizzled face. His Marine flat-top, composed of rigid silver spikes, stood in defiance of the chemo. He looked down at his muscled forearms and strong hands. The thin tubes attached to his right arm contrasted with his aged, tan skin and faded Eagle, Globe and Anchor tattoo. He looked down with pride at the lines of his fit torso through the bright white t-shirt. *Not bad for a guy in his sixties.*

He considered the irony of the disease that was eating him from the inside. He'd worked his way out of every problem life had presented so far, and for the first time, he wasn't in control of his fate. Closing his eyes, he tried to silence the noise around him. He was able to drown everything out but the endless ticking of the console. *Ademo-carcaroma, whatever they called it. Lung cancer. Fuck. Me.*

He thought about his years as a cop—the constant exposure to filth, and the infected scumbags the city had offered up. *I was young and indestructible.* He thought about the horror of the day the towers fell, and the dense wave of toxins he'd consumed. It had seemed to saturate his every pore. He thought about the people he'd saved, and those he couldn't.

I always believed I'd die heroically. Now, it'll be pathetic. He thought about the persistent nagging of his wife and son to give up the smokes. *I gave up the booze but needed my smokes. Gave them up too late.* He thought about how bored he'd become in retirement, and how he'd wished for some kind of adventure. *Be careful what you wish for.* He continued to dwell on his past selfishness and mistakes until his thoughts morphed into dreams.

A shrill beeping jolted him awake, and he bolted from the recliner with a shout. His vision sharpened; he was unsure where he was. He put his right hand where his sidearm should be and quickly scanned the room. *Who are these people?* He felt a sharp pain in his arm as the tube that led to it stretched taut. The people in the room were frozen, mouths slightly agape, staring at him. *Like mannequins in a department store window.*

He looked at the console and the flashing red words 'air-in-line.' Calming himself, he sat back down with the others in his pod—his companions in chemotherapy. He looked at the old black across the way, the biddy to his right, and the mousy Jewish guy to his left. They were all sitting in identical recliners, wired to their individual stations in the circular area. *Like hostages in an alien abduction movie.*

Nurse Carmen hustled over to fix the problem and silence the alarm in her efficient, reassuring manner. "It's alright, Chief," she said. "Stand down. I've got this under control. Lean back and relax—another half hour and you're out of here and on your way home."

He eased back into his chair. "I was dreaming, Carmen. Dreaming of better times."

The Jew looked over. "This *is* the better times. You're just starting treatment. You'll be good today, but oh boy, wait until tomorrow and the next few days!"

Tommy leaned toward the man with menace. "Who's talking to you? Shut the hell up, Herbie."

The Jew pushed backed into his chair. "Eddie. Eddie Silver. Don't be mad. There's no sugar-coating it. We're all in this together. We have to *own* it, my therapist says."

The biddy had put her celebrity gossip magazine down, now more interested in the drama a few feet away.

Tommy tried hard to suppress the prejudice that had been burned into him all his life. He saw himself as a better man now. *Except sometimes, when I'm angry.*

"Silver, huh? You mean Silverstein? Who do you people think you're fooling with the name changes? What's next, putting hair on that yama-cap of yours so nobody can see it? Don't talk about owning anything if you're faking it. Be who you are. Own *that*."

The biddy put her finger up, as if about to dispense a pearl of wisdom, until a look from Tommy silenced her.

"Yarmulke. It's a yarmulke," Eddie said quietly in response.

The tall black man regarded Tommy casually and then said in a rumbling, authoritative tone, "That's enough of that. It's bad enough in here. We're all getting through it, and we don't need any bullies. And none of that 'you people' stuff."

To hell with them. Tommy turned back to his personal TV. To discourage any further discourse, he unfurled his earbuds and plugged them into the recliner's audio port. As soon as he did, he saw the biddy and the Jew start yammering at each other and occasionally looking his way. The black gazed at him, unyielding.

He focused on the news: a story about a cop who was in trouble for shooting an unarmed young black kid who wouldn't follow instructions. The usual civil-rights leaders were getting their fifteen minutes of airtime.

Prejudice, huh? They don't understand. It's not prejudice, it's a survival instinct. When you're out there surrounded by black kids with guns under their shirts, dying to pop a cap in a cop, it's survival. They don't understand—it's not racism. Experience tells you what to be afraid of, and when to be careful. Prejudice means 'prejudge,' what's wrong with that? Isn't it how we're wired, to survive? They're not out there on the line every day in a hostile environment like I was.

He thought about his partner, his best friend, shot dead in a bodega while getting them both lunch. *Sat on my ass in the car, while Paulie's getting us sandwiches and getting killed by some lousy son of a bitch.*

The next news story rotated through, and the camera zoomed in on the talking head, whose expression was unusually grim.

"We've received an insider tip that an unnamed area priest has been accused of molesting several youths. We've reached out to the archbishop, who, citing church policy, has declined to name the priest in order to protect his reputation."

Unaware of his volume because of the headphones, Tommy said to himself angrily, "Reputation? A child molester needs to protect his reputation? The dirty rotten bastard."

He noticed the others staring at him and waved them off. The news had moved on to a story about a financial adviser who'd bilked elderly people out of their life savings. *Filthy scum. We're a plague on this planet, our species. We're a walking, talking, greedy and corrupt disease to ourselves and nature.* And then one about a politician caught philandering. *Maybe they weren't in love anymore.*

The last story brought him back to Margie, the good wife. *Or she used to be, before she turned stone cold from everything that happened, like I did. Who could blame her?* In the beginning, they were all young cops and wives, full of life. Everyone was with their first spouses, having their first kids. They were happy and naïve, and there were fun parties and card games on the weekends. No one was sick, several generations of their families were intact. No one was dead yet.

It was before the inevitable wreckage of all their lives. Their social drinking turned to self-medicating drinking. It became a problem. He gave it up; she pretended to.

His thoughts turned to the boy, their son. *Maybe I was too hard on him. He wasn't cut out to be a cop, but I pretty much mandated it. He wanted to be a writer. The kid tried to please, but couldn't hack the streets and ended up as a desk jockey. 'Secretary,' I called him. Who could blame him for hating me?* He made a note to spend more time with Bobby, to try to repair the damage in their relationship.

He realized he was feeling bad about the earlier exchange with his fellow patients. He looked them over again. They were lost in their thoughts. *Probably wondering how much time they have left in this shitty world and what they're going to do with it.* The black stared straight ahead at nothing, as if in proud acceptance of his situation. *Poor bastards.*

He didn't want them to be afraid of him; he was trying to change. *I'm a lion without teeth now.*

The biddy's husband had joined her, and he looked even frailer than she did. He'd brought her a steaming cup of tea from the cafeteria and put it on the tray next to her. They sat looking at each other wistfully, slight smiles on their lips. Their hands were intertwined, and the translucent, wrinkled, liver-spot speckled skin and bulging purple veins made it difficult to determine where one of them ended and the other began.

The Jew—Eddie—now had his small son next to him, coloring a picture as the father looked on adoringly. Tommy wondered if the boy had been nearby during his attack on the father, and the thought horrified him.

Nurse Carmen, the beautiful Nurse Carmen, was moving among them. She checked each of their infusion units and IVs to ensure all was in order. Nurse Beulah was at another pod, entertaining the patients while dancing from one to another. *How do these nurses do it every day?*

He pulled his ear buds out and stood, holding onto the infusion unit with one hand. The group looked up to see what he would do next, and there was a bit of fear in all of their faces, except the black's. The boy stopped coloring. The steam seemed to stop rising from the tea. The infusion machines kept clicking. He moved over to the Jew.

"Hello, Eddie. My name is Tommy. I'm sorry if I offended you. I'm a bit shook up about all this."

Eddie Silver smiled, and it was a nice smile— warm and friendly.

"I think I upset you by being blunt," Eddie said. "I'm like that, to a fault. It's a Jew thing."

The group laughed at the remark.

"This is my boy Saul."

The boy looked up, shook Tommy's offered hand, and went back to his coloring. Next, Tommy moved across to the biddy and her husband.

"I'm sorry, ma'am. My name is Tommy. I didn't mean to be rude earlier."

She released her husband's hand, and a wrinkled index finger came up to make her point. "I'm Helen. Helen Rosencranz. And that's alright, young man. Back in our day, people were a little more polite, but we forgive you. Herb and

I know things are different now, unfortunately. Why…"

Oh Jesus, a chatterbox. He put his hand out for the husband. "Tommy." The husband took it, and Tommy was careful not to use his normal iron grip.

"My name is Herb. It's nice to meet you, sir." He looked over at his wife, who now glared at him in disapproval for talking over her.

Tommy pulled his gear over to the black and put out his hand. He was still relaxed from his handshake with the elderly Herb, and the black squeezed firmly, bundling Tommy's fingers together. Tommy pulled his hand away.

"Let's try again. I'm Tommy." This time their two hands came to equal terms.

They looked into each other's eyes, and the man spoke his name: "Moses."

Eddie perked up. "Moses! What a great name! Yeah! Old Testament all the way, my brother!" The others looked at him with amusement.

"Moses was white," Tommy said.

"And how the hell do you know that, because all the white man books show it that way?" Moses asked, glaring at Tommy.

"Could've been black, we don't know..." Eddie interjected, trying to calm things down.

"What's the matter, Tommy—never been this close to a black man that isn't cuffed?"

Tommy cracked a hardened smile. "What's the matter with you, never been this close to a cop when you weren't?"

Moses scoffed. "Nurse Beulah, get me a copy of *Jet* or *Ebony*. Not for me, for the racist cop here. He needs to brush up on his black culture."

"And I need some Purell," Tommy called out with a smile.

With that, they all finally laughed. Moses looked at Tommy again and asked, "You saved the best for last, going to the others before coming here to me?"

"Hell, you're way over here in the back of the bus."

"Not funny," Moses said solemnly, and then smiled broadly. "You're some piece of work, Tommy. I like to think the ones who come in here angry are the ones who're most afraid."

"You got me there, brother Moses." Tommy moved back to his seat.

The boy put his crayon down and shouted, "Mister! Hey, mister!"

Tommy looked over at him. He held the picture up. It was a drawing of a cop with a gun drawn, and a robber on the ground with Xs in his eyes.

"When you were sleeping, Nurse Carmen told us you used to be a policeman, and you got shot. I drawed this picture of you." Scrawled across the top, it said 'Tommy' and at the bottom, in small, crooked print, 'By Saul Silver.' He got up and handed the picture to Tommy. "It's for you," he said.

Tommy took the picture and roughed up the boy's hair. "Yeah, kid. *Used to be* is right. I have a son, too. Now he's a big, strong policeman, just like I used to be." He sat back down and placed the drawing on his tray, then picked it up and looked at it again. Glancing over at the boy, he said, "Thank you, Saul. It's great. I'm gonna put it in my office at home."

The boy smiled. Tommy saw Moses craning to see the picture and was thankful the boy hadn't portrayed the robber as a black man.

"It wasn't me," Moses said, and they all laughed.

Tommy addressed the group. "I've been on the street long enough to know that scum comes in all colors and creeds. I was an equal-opportunity cop: I hated everyone the same."

The group were paying rapt attention and laughed nervously. "Humans are worse than most other species. Even animals don't kill their own like we do. Color don't matter. Black on black, white on white, all too common."

Moses took his turn. "I've been on the other side of that. I've made mistakes and done my time, and I'll die with a guilty conscience because of my actions and decisions. I work with street kids now, trying to make a difference. But it doesn't help things when the white cops come in with their minds already made up. Those kids don't think they have a chance and don't get the leeway white kids do when they make the same mistakes. That cop in the news shot the black kid, killed him. The kid didn't even have a weapon on him. Cop didn't even get disciplined."

"That *kid* robbed a liquor store and beat the clerk almost to death with his own bat," Tommy said.

"Doesn't mean the police have a right to shoot him dead," Eddie interjected. The biddy and her husband nodded in agreement. Saul continued to color, oblivious.

"You boys play nice now, or it's time-out for the both of you," Nurse Carmen interjected.

Tommy and Moses both turned toward their own TV monitors. "World's going to shit anyway. There's no morality anymore, black or white," Tommy said to himself.

"That much I'll give you," Moses replied.

Nurse Carmen came over to disconnect Tommy. "Okay tough guy, you're about done here for this round."

He gazed at her face and took note of every beautiful detail. Her eyeliner was perfect and straight. *Not excessive, like some of those sluttier looking women today.* The whites of her eyes were pure, the browns and green flecks in her irises reflective and sparkling. The highlights in her deep brown hair shone in the sunlight coming through the window, like strands of gold in her neat ponytail.

She went about her business, cleaning the wound with a cold alcohol swab and expertly applying a small bandage. He enjoyed her every grazing touch on his skin.

When she was through, he looked around at the others and said, "Well, I guess I'll see you folks same time, same channel in a few weeks. The missus is waiting in the chow hall downstairs."

They all said variations of goodbye as he rose up out of his chair and gathered his things. He was surprised to find his spirits and mood changed much for the better since he'd first arrived, and had a sense of camaraderie with his fellow patients. He was feeling a little bit at home.

That wasn't so bad. Maybe I can beat this damn thing.

3 CAFETERIA

TOMMY ATTEMPTED TO ENTER the hospital cafeteria against a wave of hurried employees clad in pastel scrubs depositing trays on a conveyor belt.

"This is the exit. Entrance is over there," one said, gesturing with her chin.

He weaved upstream in the direction indicated until he could finally enter the cavernous dining room. Conducting an orderly visual search, he finally spotted Margie, sitting alone. She was picking at her plate while reading a celebrity gossip magazine. He hoped she was somehow in good spirits as he took the seat facing her.

"Hi, honey, how's the salad?"

"Fine," she replied, without looking up at him. "How was your treatment?"

"It was okay. I saw the doc, too. He said that after this round, he has a clinical trial that I can try. It's worked well against this type of cancer."

She didn't answer, and he wondered if she cared. "Anyway, that's some crew of screw-ups up there, and it's depressing. Good thing you stayed down here to pass the time. Let's go."

She pulled a cherry tomato from her fork with her lips and said, between squishy bites, "Can I finish my meal, please? You should eat. You'll wake up sick tomorrow and won't want anything all day."

He hated when she talked with her mouth full, or when anyone did, for that matter. He thought about how their relationship had settled into a well-worn rut. *We're just...maintaining.*

He stewed over her disinterest as he waited. "Let me ask you something, Margie. Do you give a shit, at all?"

She finally looked up at him. "About what?"

He felt that was answer enough, but exploded at her anyway. "About me. About me being sick. About us. About any damn thing."

"Of course I do," she said levelly, before returning to her salad. "I married you, didn't I?"

He sensed that he'd gained the attention of others, and brought his voice down. "What happened to us? We used to have fun. You enjoyed life, Margie. Now you're like some goddamn robo-wife."

She picked at the plate, and he wondered if she was eating so slowly to antagonize him. *Or maybe she'd just rather be anywhere than home.*

She turned a page in her tabloid and responded, in a barely audible voice, "You used to be fun too, Tommy. That was then. This is now. Everything changes."

He decided to let it go and passed the time by watching a nearby family gorge themselves on junk food. Between mouthfuls, they sucked on straws that barely poked from the tops of their massive soda cups.

"Get a load of this crew. All overweight, the whole gang of them, kids and all. Probably regular cola, too, not even bothering with diet. No discipline."

Margie ignored him, stabbing at her salad.

The family pushed their chairs back with loud scrapes and grabbed their drinks, leaving behind a table strewn with trash.

Tommy leaned toward the father as he walked past. "Excuse me, do you think you could clean up after yourselves?"

The man paused, and his tribe came to a halt behind him. They reminded Tommy of those wobbly Russian dolls that fit inside one another.

The man swiveled his head toward Tommy and sucked the last of his drink. He prolonged the abrasive sound, while his eyes bulged from the effort. He squinted and planted his cup on Tommy's table with a rattle of ice. "How about you get that for us, pal?"

Enraged, Tommy began to rise. Margie grabbed his sleeve without looking up from her magazine. "No, sit down, or you'll end up getting arrested."

He dropped back into his seat, and the family moved on. "This is why every citizen should have to spend a few years in the Corps after high school like I did. People would learn some discipline, respect, and integrity. Damn, what a fine country we'd have."

Margie finished, and they got up to leave, dutifully clearing off their table. They walked in silence, and as they reached the parking lot, he noticed the obese family struggling into their decrepit car. The vehicle was parked sloppily in its space, too close to the one parked next to it. The wife and daughter were attempting to wedge themselves into the front and back seats, pushing their doors against the neighboring car. The vehicle, Tommy realized, was his own prized Buick.

He sprinted up as they closed the doors. He examined the side of his vehicle and saw it was scuffed, but not dented. He peered into the family's car as the father cranked the ignition and the vehicle started in ragged spurts. They seemed amused, and he lost it, rapping the top of the vehicle.

"What the fuck is wrong with you bastards? Get out, I want your insurance information!" he shouted, as the car backed up with a knock and a rattle.

The wife rolled down her window and said, "It'll buff out." They all laughed as they pulled away.

Tommy kicked the rear panel as it passed him and pulled out a pad and pen from his jacket pocket to jot down the license plate.

Margie stood on the passenger side of their car, waiting for him to unlock the doors, and shook her head. "Nothing is going to happen, you know that. Don't waste your breath and your energy."

He hit the unlock button on the key fob and opened the door for her. As he backed from his space, he spotted two extra-large soda cups next to their car, along with fragments of glass from a run-over bottle and the contents of an emptied ashtray. "Lazy sons-a-bitches," he said under his breath, as he placed his vehicle back into park.

After he'd disposed of the trash, they continued their journey home. On the highway, a vehicle approached from behind and slotted in just off his rear bumper. "Now what the hell is this, some bum is right on my ass! I'm in the right lane doing the limit plus five, what's his problem?" he asked.

Margie continued to read, oblivious.

He tapped the brakes a few times, causing Margie's head to bob forward in response, and she glared at him.

"Stop it, Tommy! What if he's some nut with a gun? Stop acting like a crazy person and let him pass when he gets a chance."

"I have a gun too—right in there," he said, gesturing toward the glove box. "Boom. Problem solved."

"Well, you aren't a cop anymore. You can't go getting into shoot-outs on the highway. Besides, what about me? What about the safety of your wife?"

Her voice had taken on the shrill tone it always had when she got worked up. *Now I'm in for it. She won't shut up the rest of the way home.*

The passing lane beside them opened up. The other vehicle swerved into it and flew by, the driver gesturing to Tommy with his middle finger. Tommy waved in response, and said, "Have a nice day, citizen." *How I loved to say that, back in my cop days.*

A few minutes later, he noticed a car on the side of the road, its front tire flattened. Four people stood staring at it as if waiting for it to inflate on its own. Tommy honked his horn, then slowed down and waved as he passed the family, pressing the button to lower Marge's window.

"Ha ha! There you go! Get some exercise fixing your tire! Karma's a bitch!" he shouted, although they were long past by the time he got it all out.

"They can't hear you, you lunatic," Margie said, as he rolled up her window and her voice came into focus once again. "What's wrong with you lately? You're losing control of yourself. I'm going to mention this to your doctor. You need something to keep you calmer, or you're going to have a stroke, never mind this cancer."

Her beehive hairdo was now in frayed disarray from the rush of wind. He tried not to laugh at the sight as he considered her question for a few minutes.

"I guess I'm afraid I'm going to leave this shitty world without having made much of a difference when assholes like them are still here to make everybody else's day worse. I tried to do that by becoming a cop, and I'm the one that's sick. Not those bastards—or these corrupt priests, lawyers, politicians, financial advisers. Me, good old Tommy, I got the cancer. Let's get home, I'm starting to feel it hitting me."

4 SICK

HE DREAMED he was back on the boat. It was the summer when Paulie had talked him into going out to night-fish for blues. They had done more drinking than fishing, and he spent the trip nauseated and retching into the sea.

As he woke, he realized he was on the living room couch, just as sick as he was that summer night. He rolled off and onto his knees, scrambling like a crab to the bathroom.

He gripped the toilet seat and emptied himself into the bowl. He had a moment to gasp and suck in air, and then it came again, and again. His convulsions were so violent that he imagined the tumors within him dislodging and flowing out with the vomit. *No such luck.*

He flushed the toilet, then crawled back to the couch and pulled the blanket over himself. *How did the blanket get here? Must have been Marge.* He became aware of a sickening smell. *Bacon.*

"I'm making you a nice breakfast. You need to keep your strength up," she yelled to him over the sounds of sizzling food and the scraping of a spatula on a frying pan.

"Please, for the love of God, no bacon. No food. Sick. Sick, sick, sick. Make it go away. Now, please." He rolled over on his stomach and buried his face in a pillow, breathing through its lavender fabric-softener fragrance. He wondered whether she'd cooked the food out of love or vindictiveness.

He woke again. It was lighter in the room and quiet, but the scent of bacon still hung in the air. She was gone. He struggled to his feet, was immediately overcome with nausea, and repeated the earlier routine.

When he was through, he went to the kitchen and took one each of the battery of pills arranged in small orange plastic bottles. There was a note from her. "Food in fridge. Please eat." *Fuck that.* He grabbed the remote before collapsing back on the couch and pointed it at the TV. He put on the news channel and then dozed off again.

"You okay, Dad?"

Opening one eye, he saw his son's bulky frame in the overstuffed recliner. "Been better, Bobby. You get the plate on the truck that hit me?"

Bobby flipped through channels with the remote control. His legs extended well beyond the footrest, and his body filled the width of the chair. *So much size, to no advantage.* He looked at the badge affixed slightly off-kilter on the rumpled uniform. *Why is he so sloppy? I was always ship-shape and crisp as a new dollar.* He noted the cowlick standing out from the back of his hair, something they'd both been unable to tame. It was one of the few recognizable remnants of the little boy he'd raised and mentored from birth.

"How's things back at the station?" Tommy asked. "You considering getting out from behind that desk and doing some real police work? You'll get some exercise on the beat, and maybe lose a few pounds. Win-win."

"It's not my deal, Pop. That was your deal. I make a difference behind the desk. I'm doing Internet-based investigation. Times have changed."

"Yeah, they have, but we still need cops on the street—boots on the ground. There's too much garbage out there, getting away with way too much. You aren't fixing that on the Internet. Don't you get pissed about the bullshit going on in this world? Don't you want to get out on the beat and make more of a difference, like me and your granddad?"

A commercial was playing for a local martial arts studio. A man with a patch on one eye was imploring the audience to come for free trial lessons. Tommy glanced over at his son to see if he was paying attention.

"Good old Sensei Molletier. That guy is a badass. You should go back to him. He had you in shape. You still have your black belt, kid."

"That was almost twenty years ago, Dad. I was twelve then. Besides, he was an abusive sadist. I think that girl in my class took his eye out with her fingernail on purpose. Everyone hated him."

Tommy paused and spoke more to himself than his son. "Yeah, I guess that's the thing now. What we used to call discipline is now called abuse. Everybody is soft these days."

His son didn't answer. "What happened to you, Bobby? I mean…back then, when you were a kid, you were into everything. Sports, fishing, hunting, Scouts, church…then you just seemed to go into some kind of shell, lost interest in everything. You were on your way to Eagle Scout, for chrissakes."

Bobby cut him off, and his voice rose. "Things happen. People change. Am I not man enough for you, Dad?"

Tommy felt his anger rise along with his son's. "Man enough? You live at home. You got no girl. You sit in your room doodling, reading comics and playing video games. You work behind a desk. Jesus. Sometimes I wonder if you're not some kind of goddamn f…"

Bobby rose from the recliner and loomed over his father. "What? A what? Go ahead, say it, Dad. A what?"

Tommy motioned him to sit down. "Okay, okay, sorry. Stop, I'm damn sick today. Please sit down, Bobby, before I puke again. Everything is okay. I'm sorry." *Maybe I'll have grandsons that I can do all that stuff with. Maybe they'll have his size, but ambition and toughness.*

He let time pass and tried to inject some humor. "I'd like to get back out there on the street and kick some ass. Maybe take Sensei Molletier with me, I'm sure he'd like that. We'd be like the Green Hornet and Kato."

"Jesus, Dad. You did make a difference. Your time is done, old man. Give up your vigilante dreams. There will always be bad guys. Nobody's going to change that. You tried. You did your part. Now relax and focus on your health and your retirement."

Tommy opened his mouth to respond but noticed Bobby was no longer listening. He'd switched to a video game involving cops and car thieves. Tommy couldn't tell which role his son was playing.

"Jesus. Seriously?" he said, before rolling back over and covering his head with the pillow.

ALMOST OUT

AS THE EARLY EVENING DARKNESS slowly took hold over his bedroom, Bobby stared up from his bed at the celestial glow-in-the-dark stickers on the ceiling. *Dad and I put them up there so long ago.*

He thought about how he'd escaped into that imaginary galaxy through all of his childhood, and still into adulthood. To a place where people didn't hate each other for being different. A place where there was only love, and no hate. A place free of greed and envy. *I called it Bobtopia. It's still out there somewhere. It's sure not here on this planet.*

He stretched out on his bed and put his hands back behind his head to relax as the light in the room diminished, and the stars slowly came alive. They called to him, and he reimagined the trip he'd taken so many times before. He closed his eyes and visualized himself strapped into an interstellar ship, taking off, leaving behind a beautiful-looking blue-and-white swirled planet that was actually rancid with an ugly populace. *Can't wait to get to Bobtopia…*

He woke as the downstairs door slammed and he heard someone stumble, followed by a shouted expletive.

"Mom, that you?" he called. "You need help?" He knew. It was the same drill, over and over. *So sick of this.*

"No, honey," she responded. "Mommy just had a little whoopsie."

And about a quart of scotch, he added to himself. *Sounds like she's really been into it this time.*

"Where's your father?" she asked.

"He said he needed something from the drugstore and went out." He heard her open the hall closet and put away her coat. He listened as first one, then a second clunk sounded to announce her shoes hitting the floor. Then came the sound he dreaded at this part of the routine, her coming up the stairs to repeat conversations they had often, she rarely remembered, and which hardly ever ended well.

She paused in the doorway to steady herself, then entered and fixed her hair in the mirror on his wall. She continued to his bed, and he quickly moved his legs aside and out of her way as she plopped down. "What's my little Bobby boo-boo doing in bed so early? Not feeling well?" She moved to feel his forehead, and he intercepted the gesture midway.

"Taking a nap, Mom. I'm on night-shift now, remember? Please don't talk to me like I'm five years old."

"Oh, right. How's work then, honey?" She rubbed his legs as they talked. It was something she'd always done back in the good times, and it eased his annoyance at her a little.

"It sucks. I never wanted to be a cop. You know that. I don't know why I ever let Dad push me into it. I think I'm going to quit."

"Oh, no. What will you do?"

He decided to probe her again, although all of his previous attempts had been rebuffed. "I'm thinking about moving out West. People are nicer there. I want to be one of those guys that sits on the sidewalk by the beach and makes paintings with spray-cans for the tourists. Maybe open an art shop and call it Bobtopia."

She erupted in laughter, and he felt his anger rise. He pushed her hand from his leg. He took his gaze from her and moved it back to the peaceful star field above.

"Do you know what I mean about being accepted, Mom? I can't be myself here, and I can't spend my life in this room wishing I could be myself."

As he anticipated, she ignored the prod. "Now, honey. You won't leave me, will you? It would be just Daddy and me. We'd be so lonely in this house without you."

"You obviously don't see the irony in that statement, Mom. I thought you were going to quit drinking? You reek. You told Dad and me you'd stop. Time after time, you told us. You're silly when you're drunk, and cranky when you're not." He sensed her mood change as his comments hit their mark, and he knew that now she'd go on the defensive.

"You listen here, young man. I have a lot to deal with. Your father is sick. I need a little time for myself. The only downtime I get is when I can spend time with my sister."

"Don't bring the cancer into this, Mom. It's been a problem for long before that. Don't use it as your excuse. Maybe you and Dad would get along better if you would just stop."

Her voice rose. "Did you ever think that maybe I drink because of your father? Do you know how hard it's been to be married to a cop? To a man like him? Why do you defend him? I've always been there for you!"

"Yes, I know. It's always been good cop and bad cop with you two. He was tough on me. It helped me a lot."

"He was brutal to us both. Remember when he was drunk, coming home from that bar after work, how mean he was to us?"

"I do remember. It's a tough job. A lot of pressure. I know that firsthand now. Grandpa was the same way to him. Even worse, actually, from what I remember and the stories Dad told me. At least he's changing now, though. He's trying. You need to try, too."

"So he gets a pass, Bobby, and I'm the bad guy now?"

The booze wafting through the room from her breath offended him. This space was his sanctuary, and he never drank much because of the violence it had always caused in their home.

"He never cheated on you, Mom. I know that. He never crossed that line." He added an accusatory tone toward the end of his statement to her, and he could tell she picked up on it by the fear that came across her face.

"Well, I don't do anything wrong. I just spend time with Aunt Diane to get away from everything for a little while. That's all."

"Really, Mom?"

"Yes. It's just social time. She and I like to have a few drinks to unwind."

"And that's what you were doing today?"

"Yes, just like I said. I'm your mother. Don't question me."

"Okay, because she called about an hour ago looking for you. This is a real house of lies, isn't it?"

"Don't you dare…," she started to say, before rising up and going to her bedroom, closing the door firmly behind her.

It was fully dark, and the far-away galaxy now sparkled brightly above him. He closed his eyes again and turned on his side to face the wall and return to his dreams.

6 BUSTER VELA

MOSES CAME INTO the infusion area, and Tommy suppressed his happiness at seeing the man. He took the station next to Tommy instead of his usual place directly across. The TV was tuned to the news.

"What's up, my brother?" Moses asked.

Tommy leaned back in his chair to eyeball his antagonist, feigning resentment. "Brother? If we are, it's damn sure from another mother."

Moses laughed a deep, rich laugh. Tommy couldn't help but laugh as well, and soon both were coughing hard and trying to regain control.

This caught the attention of Nurse Carmen, who hustled over to confront them. "What's all the commotion about over here, you two?" she asked, with her hands on her hips and a motherly expression.

The two gave her blank stares, then looked at each other and started laughing again.

"Frick and Frack, I do swear. You two behave, or I'm sending you down for electroshock."

The men laughed even harder at the suggestion.

"Are you two ready for insertion?" she asked, waving the IV needle.

"Do it to me, baby," Tommy responded.

Carmen continued to admonish the men as she inserted their IVs and began their drips. They watched as Carmen moved off to check on another patient. Both pairs of eyes followed her, focused in particular on the form-fitting bottom of her hospital scrubs.

"Ain't that a sight to behold?" Tommy said.

Moses cast his eyes down. "At my age, they all look the same to me. But ain't nobody can hold a candle to my Angie, God rest her soul," Moses said. "Angie, my angel, I always used to tell her."

Tommy sensed the man's guilt for having looked at all. "How old you figure she is?"

Moses rubbed his chin. "Hard to tell sometimes with the Latinos and Asians, they got good skin. I'd say forties maybe."

"Yeah," Tommy added. "One give-away is the elbows. Some women spend so much on all that plastic surgery and Botox, but the elbows are like the rings on a tree stump. She doesn't look it at all, but I'm thinking maybe late forties. She's got wisdom and maturity that comes with age, too."

"You got a thing for her, I can tell," Moses said. "But you're wearing a ring, Chief. You got something special back home, so you're only window-shopping, right? Ain't no harm in that. Nurse Carmen's not wearing one. Too bad you're not available."

"That's a tough one, Moses. You know how it goes. I guess there are those fairy-tale marriages where people grow old together and stay in love. Maybe. Or maybe those people are as bored with each other as me and my old lady, just good at faking it. Maybe they're fooling their selves. To be honest, we were talking about calling it quits, and then I got sick. But yeah, that Carmen, she floats my boat. Not that an old-timer like me would have a shot."

They were quiet for a while, lost in their own thoughts while the poison crept through their vessels. Tommy thought back to his early years with Margie. Their first chapters were fun and adrenaline-filled. He was a beat cop, coming back to home-cooked meals. She reveled in his stories of the adventures that had occurred on his shift. They socialized with the other cops and spouses—grand drunken parties and card games, to blow off steam and the stress of the job.

And then things changed. His partner died, her parents died, and in the course of a single year, a permanent cloud of darkness seemed to descend on them.

Little Bobby appeared on the scene, along with the added stress and expense of parenthood. The job got tougher as Tommy grew older and took on more responsibility. He grew hardened and cold from the experiences it brought him.

Margie had grown in turn into a jaded cop wife. Drinking went from fun to necessary, and then to a dependency for both of them. They went for help together.

He gave it up; she claimed to, and he learned to ignore the fact that she hadn't. He let her think she was doing a good job of hiding it. Despite his attempts to bring Bobby up with the discipline he'd learned in the Corps, the boy became lazy and sloppy, adding to the conflict in the home.

And then he retired, got sick, and everything became even worse.

He realized the incessant drone of the news on his TV was adding to his declining mood, and turned it to the sports channel. They were just getting to the hockey highlights. "Good timing," he said to himself.

Moses craned his neck to look over. "I could never get that sport. Can't follow the damn ball."

"Oh, come on. And it's called a puck. Okay, what do you like?"

"Hoops, baseball, football."

"Okay, in baseball and football, how the hell often do you actually see the ball? Hoops, shit. African ballet, my old man used to call it."

Instead of laughing this time, Moses glared at him, offended. "Now I see where you get it from, cracker. Chip off the old block, ain't you? Your pappy wear a white hood on the weekends? You're crossing a line with that African ballet shit. Look here, you see any brothers on the ice? That's some racist shit there."

"Alright, alright. I'm sorry, it was the old man's way. Things are different now. I'm different too. Times have changed. We can't do anything about the ignorance of the past." He gestured to the screen. "As for this, your people need to learn to skate. I'm sure they'd be happy to have you."

They laughed again. Moses continued to watch. "So that's the Rangers, right? Red, white and blue like the good ol' US of A. Our team?"

Tommy was happy for the reach-out, and said, "Yeah, that's our guys there. And I guess I'm a Knicks fan now?"

Moses chuckled more subtly this time to keep his damaged lungs in check. "Hell no! Nets all the way. Remember Dr. J? Now he was the man, oh yeah. Now you got me all worked up, and I got to piss."

Moses stood and moved with his rig towards the men's room. Nurse Carmen came over to check on Tommy. "How's it hanging, Chief? Where'd your buddy go, you finally ran him off?"

"He's in the head. I'm doing alright over here. You sure this thing is working? You're not giving me decaf, are you?"

Carmen laughed as she moved closer to adjust the knobs on the unit. She smelled good to Tommy. She was leaning forward enough while adjusting the equipment for him to see down the front of her blouse. The sight of the white lacy brassiere against her mocha skin sent shock waves through his groin that he hadn't felt in a long time.

He imagined kissing her, as he glanced from her cleavage and her smooth brown cheeks and full lips. He'd always had a thing for the Latinos, because of his sense of duty and morals he'd never taken advantage of his opportunities. *Look where that got me.*

He imagined she was doing this to get a reaction from him. Maybe she was lonely. He had to take a shot, or he'd go home full of regret, like the time he almost asked Ginny Paoli to dance at sophomore homecoming. He went for it, with the directness that a cop learns.

"Nurse Carmen, you sure smell good. What's a good-looking, caring, wonderful-smelling woman like you doing without someone special to go home to? If a man like me were to find himself on the market, do you think you'd consider dinner with him?"

She continued her work without even looking at him, and said dismissively, "I got my man, Chief. He's my world, and takes away all the pain I bring home from this job. I don't wear my rings on the job; I don't want them to be scratching and poking my patients, and don't want them slipping off. We have to wash up a hundred times a day. Too many close calls. Now you sit there, get better, and stop hitting on the staff."

The pangs of rejection erased the earlier tingling. Feeling sad and sick, he turned the channel back to the news. *Shouldn't have tried that.* He hadn't noticed that Moses had come back and was sitting next to him again.

Nurse Carmen reached up to adjust the IV bag, and they both looked up as her shirt stretched and exposed the frilly bra beneath it. It also exposed a deep purple-and-green bruise in the shape of fingers around her bicep. She finished and moved away.

"Strike one, two, and three!" Moses said.

Tommy looked at him with concern. "You see that shit? The bruise on her arm? I've seen it before, lots of times. Somebody had a hell of a grip on her. Son of a bitch."

"Enter the bad guy," Moses said, looking across the room.

Tommy followed his gaze. Carmen was engaged in discussion with a large Latino man in ragged, dirty jeans and a black t-shirt. He was angry and glaring in Tommy's direction. She was trying to move him away and keep him calm.

Moses grunted. "I don't think he liked what he saw when she was over here with you, you looking down her shirt and all."

Tommy stared defiantly back at the man. He tried to send a message with a glare—*Do not hurt that woman, or you will pay.* Carmen pulled her purse from the counter, said something to Nurse Beulah, and manipulated the man out of the door.

Tommy stood, moved his rig over to the window, and waited. As he expected, a short time later he saw them both emerge from the building and head into the parking lot. "There they go," he said.

Curious, Moses got up and moved over next to him. They watched the two approach a battered old Ford.

The man pulled Carmen over to the passenger side, yanked the door open, and shoved her in, then went around and got in the driver's side. A few moments later, puffs of blue smoke emerged from the exhaust, and the vehicle sped from the lot.

Tommy took note of the plate and pulled his notebook from his shirt pocket to jot it down. "Son of a bitch," he said.

"Those two are always going at it. It's nothing. That's love, I guess—at least to some people." The two turned and saw Nurse Beulah looking on behind them. "You two sit down, you're both about done. Let me get this stuff off you."

When they'd been relieved of their tubes, the two walked down the hall to the elevator together. They entered, and Moses pressed the button for the ground floor. "I don't know about you, whitey, but I need a drink. Care to join me?"

"Sure. I'll drive, but I ain't drinking."

"You saying black folk don't have cars?"

Tommy laughed. "I'm saying I haven't observed you ever coming in with any car keys on your person. Empty-handed and flat-pocketed, except for the wallet in your back left."

"Damn, busted. You cops are always in surveillance mode. Yeah, a lift home after might be good. I got a place I like, just a few blocks away. Walking distance. I thought your old lady usually came with you to drive you back?"

"I guess that was a one-time sympathy thing. Apparently, I'm on my own now."

7 WYLA'S BAR

MOSES LED THE WAY. They traveled down the city streets, cutting through back alleys.

As the surroundings became more decrepit, Tommy became more uncomfortable. He knew he'd left his carry weapon in the glove box, but patted his jacket to check for it anyway. *Should've brought it into the hospital. Didn't know I'd end up in the hood.*

"Almost there," Moses said.

As soon as they rounded the corner, Tommy knew where they were headed. He remembered the place from long ago—Wyla's Bar. The same half-lit neon sign hung in warning above the entrance. He hoped nobody inside would remember him.

He followed Moses into the dim tavern. The only light came from the glow of various beer signs and video games bordering a worn black-and-white checkered floor. The place was empty, except for a large, bald black man behind the bar. They mounted two barstools.

Moses gestured to the taps. "Two drafts, Lucius. Make 'em tall."

"Coke for me. Throw some ice in it, please," Tommy added.

Lucius eyed him without moving. "I smell the law. Who you keeping company with, Mos?"

Moses put his hand on Tommy's shoulder. "He's alright. Fellow patient, he got the Big C, same shit as me. Not the law anymore. Just another guy like me with a short runway."

Lucius pulled a glass from the shelf and reluctantly filled it as the soda gun made a strangled noise.

Tommy could see the spots and grime on the glass despite the dim light in the bar.

Lucius placed it on the bar far enough for Tommy to have to reach to get to it. "Here's your pop, Pops."

"Ice, Luce," Moses said firmly.

Lucius slid an aluminum bin open and used a metal scoop to gather a few cubes. He plopped them into Tommy's glass, causing the contents to fizz and overrun the rim. "He's alright for now. But you know it's gonna get busy in here soon, and my patrons may not feel the same way. I don't guarantee anyone's safety."

Moses nodded. "Give us an hour, brother. We have some things to discuss."

Lucius moved back to his stool by the stereo system in the corner, well away from them, and placed headphones over his ears.

Moses pulled hard on the icy mug, his large hand wrapped around the handle. "So what's the deal? You a recovering drunk or something, Chief?"

Tommy sipped from the smudged glass. "Not so much. Not that bad. My old lady is the one that has a problem with it. It wasn't helping matters much when we were both hitting the sauce. At a certain point, you get old enough to figure out all it ever bought you was saying and doing things you regret the next day, or the rest of your life. Not to mention acting like a jackass, and hurting a lot of people you care about. I don't like making bad decisions, and I don't like waking up sick in the morning."

Moses laughed. "Well, you're in the wrong club then. We all have a lot of sick mornings ahead of us. You might as well take it up again."

Tommy shook his head. "Yeah, the irony of it. Ain't that a bitch."

Moses stared into the depths of his mug. "I was supposed to quit. It was a condition of my parole to stay out of places like this. Too much drinking leads me to violent tendencies, especially the hard liquor. That's what got me locked up. I much prefer the weed. It keeps me nice and mellow. But, old habits die hard."

The silent television flickering above the bar caught Tommy's attention. He read the closed captioning as the muted newscaster moved her lips.

"It has been discovered that the accused priest was convicted of child abuse many years ago when he was a Scout leader, prior to his becoming a priest. The Church admits knowledge of his past transgressions but cited canon law, which prevents him from being punished for acts that were done when he was a layman. There had

been a binding agreement between the Church and law enforcement that he was not to be placed in any role or situation where he would be around children. It is unclear whether these recent alleged acts took place in his capacity as a priest, or outside of Church activities or premises..."

"Damn!" Tommy pounded his fist on the bar, causing Lucius to rip off his headset and stand. "Can you believe this shit? The motherfucker molested kids before, and the Church knew about it!"

Lucius shook his head and went back to his music and stool.

"Yeah," Moses said. "I've been following that. Nothing changes. Church been covering up for them and moving them around forever. I remember it going on when I was a kid, but not on the news. My daddy used to be a janitor at the church. Both my parents were devout. Made me memorize the Scriptures, and I had to read the Good Book cover to cover. We didn't talk bad about the church at home. Church could do no wrong. I guess it's all about forgiveness. People with nothing need religion to lean on, to get them through the day, to give them some kind of hope that things will get better, at least after they're dead."

Tommy drained his glass and put it down, waving to Lucius that he didn't need a refill. "Right, and what the fuck is this priest doing out anyway? See, this is what I mean. Too much leniency. These perverts don't ever get rehabilitated. They got a mental defect. They should never be let out once they're caught. Anyone molests a kid should die. Or put them all on some goddamn island and let them molest each other. Now that's a son of a bitch I'd like to take out myself. If it was my kid, I'd damn sure take care of it. I don't give a goddamn if I had to spend the rest of my life in the joint."

"Easy there, cowboy," Moses said, looking into his empty mug. "He'll get what he's owed one way or another. Anyway, he fucked up again and got caught. He's goin' away for good this time, I'm sure. Let's talk about that asshole who's hurting Carmen.

"It's a hell of a thing," Tommy answered. "Something I always hated. I remember my daddy hitting on my momma. I swore I'd get him back, but I was never big enough until he was gone. Then Momma was gone, and I never forgave myself, even though I was just a kid. Ever since then, I can't stand to see it. Same damn kind of marks on Carmen's arm that my momma always had on hers. From the gripping and shaking."

Tommy swirled the ice in his glass. The door creaked open, and light flooded the room as a slim young black man, wearing a patched black leather vest and with a bandanna wrapped around his head, slid in.

Tommy followed his path as he moved to the far end of the bar and sat. Lucius poured his drink without being asked. *A regular.* He watched as they said a few things to each other. The barkeep moved back to his stool, replacing his headphones. The new patron took a casual look down the bar at them, then quickly looked away.

Tommy replied to Moses, "Ain't that something, though. Carmen spends all day busting her ass in that damn place, taking care of sick people, and then goes home to a motherfucker like that creep. I can't stand to think about her getting hit. Never could tolerate anyone hurting women or kids. Those were the busts I took the most pleasure in, back in the day."

He watched as the slim man stood, looked their way, then walked out the door, leaving a half-full drink on the bar. The intuition that had been burned into him in his years as a cop tingled. Lucius sat on his stool like a Buddha with shades and headphones, staring straight ahead.

Moses didn't seem concerned, or perhaps hadn't noticed. *He doesn't have the cop sense, he's got street sense, and this is a safe place to him.*

Moses spoke again. "You want to talk to Carmen's man? Put a little scare in his ass?"

"Yeah, what do we have to lose, Mos? We're two sick old fuckers, past our prime. Let's make a difference for her, anyway. Small thing."

"We're going to have to space it away from these treatments though," Moses said. "I don't start getting any strength back for a good while, stuff knocks the shit out of me."

"Good point. We'll set it up for just before the next round."

Lucius got up and refreshed Moses' drink, leaving Tommy's empty glass unattended. Moses was about to say something, but Tommy waved him off.

"How we gonna get to him?" Moses asked.

"Ever see that old cop movie where they send invitations out to the guys who have warrants, to meet some pro athlete and get autographs? Like they won a contest or something? *Serpico*, right? I got guys on the force still who can set it up for us on the down-low. Maybe get one of the undercover narcs to see if he'll bite on a drug buy and pickup, and get him to work the door for us."

"Where we gonna do something like that?"

"I know about some abandoned industrial properties we can use. It'll be dark, he'll never see us. He'll never suspect a couple of sick old men. Let me work on it. We'll do it for Nurse Carmen— she's our angel. One thing I learned, most of these guys who beat on their women are big pussies themselves. He'll back right the fuck down and maybe think twice next time. I'll set it up."

While they continued to hatch their plan, Tommy saw something begin to glow behind the bar.

Lucius picked up his phone and looked at it. He got up and moved from behind the bar to stand on the far side of the room, away from the door.

The situation clicked in Tommy's mind, and his aged body moved into action. *Ambush.* Rising from his barstool as the front door opened, he grabbed Moses by the arm and pulled him away. Moses' mug of beer swung wildly, splashing in a wide arc. The flood of light as the door opened was quickly blotted out by the bodies pushing through it.

"Get down, Moses! Move to the dark," Tommy shouted as he pulled his friend to the floor on the far side of the room, out of the line of attack he expected to come. He jumped in front of Moses to shield him.

The door closed, and the bodies that had rushed in encircled them. His eyes hadn't adjusted to the dark again. *I don't have my fucking weapon.* Someone grabbed him, and as a reflex, he used a judo throw. The mechanics were the same as when he was younger, but his body was less responsive. He was old but still strong, and he was able to swing his attacker away, slamming him into an arcade game, smashing the glass. *They can't see either.*

He dropped to a kneeling posture and pulled his glasses case from his jacket pocket. He aimed it as if it were a gun, swinging his extended arms in a semi-circle. "Don't fucking move or I'll unload this full fucking clip."

The lights flipped on, and Tommy saw Lucius at a row of switches by the door.

The barkeep threw the deadbolt and stood with his arms folded. "Seems like some people have a beef to settle with you, Pops."

Now they were all exposed. Tommy in the center of a ring of younger black men, all with the same leather motorcycle vests and bandannas around their foreheads. Moses sprawled on the floor behind him. Tommy crouched in a shooting posture, pointing a faux leather case from Pearle Vision like a 9mm Glock.

Several of the men laughed, but the one who'd been thrown stepped forward and slapped the case from Tommy's hand. "You ain't no cop. Not no more. Just an old man. I got a real problem with you, motherfucker."

The most muscular youth in the group walked up to Moses and extended a hand to help him up. "Uncle Moses. Sorry you got caught up in the action."

Moses straightened himself. "Goddamit Lukas, what the hell is this all about? Where are your bikes? I didn't hear you coming."

Tommy looked at Moses, then back to the group. Some held helmets. "What the fuck is this, the black Hell's Angels?"

Moses replied, "This is my nephew, Lukas. He runs with this group from our hood. Black Eagles, not Hell's Angels. It's a new group, gives 'em something to do. I'm kind of their adviser, trying to keep them out of trouble. Not easy in our neck of the woods."

Don't show fear. Tommy stood and addressed the young man who'd slapped his glasses case away. "What's your beef?"

"You took this place down. Ten years back," he replied. "They were some working motherfuckers, ain't making shit at their jobs, playing poker in the back room. My motherfucking old man. You put him away, bitch. Cost me time with him. And probably went to your own motherfucking card game with your cop buddies that same night. Time to pay your dues now. Racist motherfucking cops." He moved forward, as did the others, tightening the circle around Tommy.

"Easy fellas, easy…" Moses tried to interject.

"Stay out of it, Mos. I want to hear what he has to say," the youth commanded.

Tommy's mind raced back to that night. He remembered it. The game had started as a neighborhood thing, but it'd gotten out of control, taking in big money and starting to get the attention of the local mob. Bad for the neighborhood and the city, and bad for these poor working stiffs if the mob decided to move in. He'd wanted to do the take-down and get out without any problems. They were doing these guys a favor, but nobody knew it at the time.

But then Paulie, *fucking Paulie,* had to let his hatred get the best of him and went over the top. He went out to the car, came back, and planted weapons and weed that were never there. Added years onto what would've been weeks for the guys they busted.

Moses dared to move closer. "Now hold on a minute. None of you kids were there. I was there. Yeah, the cops took us down. We were asking for it, we were getting greedy and sloppy and taking action from out of the neighborhood. Too much attention."

"You his narc?" the leader asked Moses. "You had your time. This is our time. We got to make shit right, or we got no dignity. Price to pay for everything. That's the law of the street."

Moses came forward, towering over them all. "Learn respect, young man. I know your father taught you that, at least. I was there that night. This man was the only one trying to be fair. Shit got out of control. His partner wasn't as fair. But this man here wanted to break it up and let everyone go. He's okay. You got the wrong guy. You want someone, go after the other one."

"Fuck that. I'll take the one I can get. Proximity got a price. No cop is a good cop. Not that I seen."

Tommy addressed the man. "Listen, he's right. My partner was over the top. I always tried to be fair. He paid the price. He got popped in a bodega."

It was quiet for a moment. Tommy broke the silence first. "Look, when I was a cop, I hated everyone, including myself. I tried to be fair. I let a lot of shit go. Paulie's gone. He paid the price."

The leader pulled a knife from his cargo pants and clicked it open. "You got to pay the price. I got to remove something from you, for my daddy."

Moses stepped in front of Tommy. "Look here. You see what this man did when you came in? He put himself in front of me. He's sitting here in a brother bar, a white man, and puts his body in front of a brother when there's danger. Ain't too many white men like that. Ain't too many *cops* like that, black or white."

A distant wail grew louder as it neared, until it peaked outside the door. The young men all scrambled, and one yelled, "Back door!"

Tommy said, "Wait. Don't be stupid. It's probably covered. You go running through there, and you'll get taken down. Hold on." He looked over at Lucius. "Unlock the fucking door before they break it in."

Lucius threw the bolt back, and Tommy opened door enough to expose his face and spoke. "Stand down. The situation in here is under control."

He opened the door the rest of the way to reveal several uniformed officers. "Sergeant Borata, what the hell are you doing here?" one of them asked. "We got a report of a disturbance."

"I'm having a few beers with my friends. It's under control."

The officer appeared skeptical and peered behind Tommy to get a better view of the occupants. "Your *friends*? You sure?"

"Yeah. Just a disagreement over some sports shit. I wanted to watch the hockey game. Go get some real bad guys."

The cops turned away, and Tommy closed the door. "I got to get out of here." He reached into his wallet and threw a hundred-dollar bill on the bar. "Lucius, that's for the repairs, and get these guys a drink on us." He looked at Moses and nodded toward the door. They both left without complaint from the others, who were eyeing the cash and taking seats at the bar.

When they were outside with the door closed, Tommy turned to Moses. "You were there that night?"

Moses laughed. "Hell no. That was some spur-of-the-moment bullshit. Improvisation."

Tommy put his hand on the man's shoulder. "Jesus. You saved my ass with that. What you said wasn't far off from how it really went down."

"Yeah, good cop/bad cop. Same old story. That much I know from experience. Sorry about your partner. Was that for real?"

"Yeah, he got hit. Not blacks though. It was a white kid, junkie who was taking down a bodega, high as a kite. Paulie wasn't perfect, but he was my best friend."

They walked down the streets, avoiding the alleys this time.

"You know what, Borata? You're a dangerous motherfucker to hang around with."

"Yeah, well—let me pick the bar next time. I'm too old for this shit."

8 A WARNING

THERE WAS JUST ENOUGH light filtering through the ragged shade in the old warehouse office for them to make out each other's forms. Tommy set his Taser to 'drive-stun' mode.

"Now youse can't leave," he said, laughing.

"Huh? What the fuck does that mean?" Moses asked.

"*Bronx Tale.* You never saw that flick?"

"No, I guess I'm not as much of a movie buff as you," Moses replied. "Is that a gun?"

"Nope—a Taser. Beautiful piece of equipment, standard police issue. This little baby can be used for direct contact against the body, or shoot electrodes from fifteen feet away into the perpetrator."

"I don't know about this shit. I'm sick, Chief. Too sick to go back to jail. What if I get better, and have to spend years back in the hole? What if this motherfucker has a heart attack from that thing?"

"Nobody's going to jail. C'mon. We're both sick. We planned this out. It's not a big deal. We don't need to do much. I've got all the tools to take him down, give him a warning, and get the hell outta here. Geez. Maybe I should have gotten you drunk on some hard stuff, to bring out those violent tendencies you talked about. Think about Nurse Carmen. All she does is care for us, and then she goes home to get beat on by this asshole. You okay with that?"

"You know I'm not," Moses replied. "You sure this guy is dumb enough to come to a place like this alone?"

"Yup. I checked him out. He's pretty fucking stupid. Masks down."

They both pulled ski masks down over their faces. "We look fucking ridiculous," Moses said.

It was silent except for the thrum of the idling vehicle outside, and Tommy spoke again.

"Don't forget. When Davis out there opens the door to push him in, close your eyes until you hear the door shut behind him. Our eyes are already adjusted to the dark; his won't be. It'll be over quick, and then we're out of here. Follow our plan. It's only a warning for him."

"I don't know about this. What if he recognizes our voices?"

"He never heard us talk. It'll be okay." Tommy checked his watch, knocked on the door and asked the narc outside if he was ready.

"All set," came the muffled reply.

The men waited until the silence was broken by the sound of an approaching vehicle.

"Show-time. Buckle up," Tommy said.

Davis knocked twice from the outside, the agreed-upon signal. It was the car and driver they were expecting.

The sounds of muffled tough talk came from both men outside.

"Davis is good," Tommy whispered. "He'll convince Vela the good deal he's been promised is just inside this door."

Tommy psyched himself up to get past the pangs of nausea that wracked his stomach in waves. He remembered his poor mother, and what she'd had to endure at the hands of his father when he came home from drinking after his shift. He recalled his father's fighting advice.

When you're in it, you gotta be an animal, kid. There's no playing fair in a street fight. It's you or the other guy. Unleash the animal within you, and be vicious. The moment he fears you, you've won.

Tommy and Moses pressed themselves flat against the wall, on opposite sides of the door. Both closed their eyes, and their pulses raced. Finally, the door creaked open. Davis shoved Vela through and pulled it shut. Moses threw the deadbolt into place.

Tommy moved like a cat. The adrenaline surging through his body erased the sickness and made him feel twenty years younger. He loved it—missed its feel from his days on the street. It was the elixir of survival and strength, and he hadn't felt it in a long time.

He jabbed his Taser into Vela's ribs while he was still off-balance, and commanded, "On the ground. On the ground, *now*."

The static clicking and blue-lightning bursts of the Taser added to the kinetic electricity in the room. Vela's limbs twitched and jerked.

Moses quickly swept the man's legs out from under him. The two worked in concert to roll him onto his stomach, zip-tying his feet and arms behind him.

Buster fought, to no avail. Realizing he was beat, he started begging for mercy. "What's up? What's up, amigos? Rodriguez send you? Tell that motherfucker I'll pay him next week when my bitch gets paid. I swear. Please."

"Shut the fuck up," Tommy said. He sat on Vela's back, crushing his bound hands, then grabbed his long greasy hair and yanked his head backward. Dropping the Taser, he pulled his 9mm semi from an underarm holster beneath his jacket and pushed it to the back of the man's head.

"Easy. Easy," Moses said, holding his hands out, palms up, to Tommy.

Vela squirmed. "Don't. Don't fucking kill me! I got a kid, I got an old lady. They need me!"

Tommy yanked Vela's head back further and cocked the hammer of the weapon.

"Don't break his damn neck," Moses said anxiously.

"No! What do you want? Anything!"

Tommy leaned down next to Vela's ear and spoke in a harsh, menacing tone. "Listen up, Buster. Your old lady don't need you. You need her. You're a useless piece of shit, and lucky to have her. You ever fucking touch her again, we're gonna find you and finish the job."

"What the fuck, I didn't do nothing to her. Who sent you, her brother?" Vela asked.

"Never mind that. Maybe I'll empty this whole motherfucking clip into your greasy head. And then she'll be the luckiest old lady in the world. Your kid too. This is your last warning, *bitch*. We're gonna go now, but if you leave this building in the next ten minutes, you'll be even sorrier."

Tommy tightened his grip on the man's hair and slammed his forehead into the concrete floor. It made a sickening thud, and Moses turned away. Tommy holstered his gun and pulled a large combat knife from a sheath on his ankle.

"Jesus. Fucking Rambo, ease up," Moses said.

Tommy kicked Vela, who didn't move. "He's out cold. Let's get out of here." Tommy cut the ties on the man's legs but left his hands bound.

"At least make sure he's fucking breathing!"

Tommy knelt down, pulled the man's head back slightly, and listened. Blood dripped from Vela's forehead into a growing, glistening pool on the floor. "He's fine. Just sleeping. It won't take him long to get loose when he wakes up."

The men exited the building, shielding their eyes from the late afternoon light. Davis was already gone. Moses struggled to pull his mask and tight leather gloves off. "I feel like OJ," he said.

"Keep them on until we're out of here," Tommy said. He moved to Vela's car and stabbed a tire. It hissed and sang as the vehicle sagged down. He looked inside the car and found Vela's cell phone sitting in the cup holder. He reached inside for it, then threw it to the ground and pierced it with the knife. "Let's go."

They walked toward the back of the building, where they'd stashed their car. Halfway there, Moses buckled over and vomited. "Fucking chemo. Fuck. That's DNA there, what do we do with it?"

Tommy laughed and kicked dirt over it. The smell reached his nostrils and sent him over the top, and he could no longer hold back. He knelt in the dirt and puked, then rose and wiped his mouth with his sleeve. "He isn't going to call anything in. He's got warrants."

"Damn, then why not have him picked up instead of doing all this?"

"Because this is more fun, and more effective. The system doesn't care about petty trash like him, and he knows it. He'd be right back out and probably beat Carmen twice as bad."

The first half of the drive was silent. Tommy was spent from the effort of it, far more from the treatments than his age.

"So, what the fuck was that with the gun? What happened to sticking with the plan?" Moses asked.

"It was insurance, in case he got away from us. Anyway, I didn't have the clip in."

"Chief, that shit was excessive. I don't remember anything about busting his head either."

"Yeah, sorry. The adrenaline flows and something takes me over. Anyway, there is no *excessive* with these scumbags. I didn't want him trying anything when we were leaving. He needed a shot, to see what it's like on the other side of abuse."

"You sure about that Davis cat? Where's he at?"

"I told him to go as soon as Vela was inside. He's solid. He owes me a lot of favors, and I've got leverage over him. It's good to have people who owe you, and it's smart to have dirt on them, too."

9 THERAPY

BOBBY SAT BACK in the plush leather chair, rested his head, and closed his eyes. It was something that Dr. Eastwood had him do in order to answer questions without becoming too emotionally involved, as a sort of out-of-body experience. *I hate it here, but I love this chair...*

"It's been a while," he heard Dr. Eastwood drone. "How have you been, Bobby?"

"About the same, I guess. My old man is sick, though. Cancer."

"How does that make you feel?"

"It's funny—for most of my life, I wished he would get cancer, or get hit by a car. Now I feel guilty and pretty fucking sad about it. The guy was like the Great Santini—ever see that movie? I thought he was invincible."

While the doctor took notes and shuffled papers, he thought about his childhood. His parents in drunken arguments, him thinking he could fix everything by trying to please them any way he could, including living in denial about who he really was. He thought about being picked on in school all of those years for being overweight, effeminate, and the son of a tough cop. He'd watched his classmates fall happily in love, dance at school parties, hold hands in the hallways, be free and happy, and he couldn't have any of it himself.

"There's been a lot in the news regarding this priest lately. Do you want to talk about that yet, Bobby?"

Every time the therapist had brought it up in the past, he'd danced around the subject. The walls were thick for him, and he had a lot of practice at home living in denial that anything had ever happened. But he'd gotten tired of it, tired of not making progress in eliminating his demons, of not being open about who he was, and ultimately of not being happy. *I'm getting older; I can't live with this bottled up inside forever.* He listened to the soothing sound of the wall clock. *Tick. Tick. Tick.* Each beat seemed an eternity, and he used the time to summon his courage.

"Bobby?"

"Yeah, sorry. Okay, I can talk about it. What do you want to know? Let's get it over with."

"Start at the beginning."

Bobby ran the clock back in his mind, trying to bring forward things long since buried in the fog. He looked at the door and considered bolting.

"He picked me out. He saw that I was an awkward gay kid without any friends. I was alone most of the time at the church. My parents made me go but rarely went with me. I think my old man thought that somehow Jesus would convert me. Isn't that ironic?

"Anyway, the priest favored me, made me feel accepted, made me want to go there and hang around. Made me an altar boy. He was funny, made me laugh, and acted like a real dad, or a big brother."

"Did he acknowledge the conflict with the church's view on homosexuality?"

"Yeah, he said it was okay. Said that really we were all God's children, and he was bisexual— that he loved everyone and it was okay to love no matter how you did it. That's how it started; he said he was going to help me discover who I was, teach me stuff I would need to know for my boyfriend someday."

"You never got to confide in anyone, not your mom?"

"No. I tried a few times, hinted to my mom. She shut it down immediately. I couldn't talk to any of the counselors or teachers at the school. My old man knew everyone, and I was too scared of him finding out.

"It was just little stuff at first... It was surreal for me, as a kid. I didn't know what to do. I felt trapped, and he knew it."

"Where are you at with it now? How do you feel, aside from your other challenges?"

"With the priest? I've wanted to kill him my whole life. I became a cop because of him, really, not the pressure from my dad. I figured maybe I'd get my chance someday to put him behind bars. But I moved on, in my own denial, and never really went there. I don't like being a cop in the first place. Plus, I always worried that if I busted him, or someone else like him, things would come out about me. I remember him taking pictures. I didn't want to be embarrassed by it. Now that he's in the news, I'm terrified and stressed the fuck out every day that those things will come to light."

"Let's move past that, Bobby. What about coming out? That's one thing you do have control over. It would be hard at first, but you'd be happier in the long run."

"It's tough to imagine, especially with my old man. He's changing, though, so…maybe. I'll give it some thought."

He sat up and looked at the door again. This time he got up and went through it.

10 REMISSION

TOMMY WATCHED through the hospital window until he saw the busted-up Ford pull into the parking lot. As he anticipated, Carmen had driven herself, rather than Buster dropping her off. The donut tire had been installed. *She probably changed that herself.*

He continued to watch as she emerged from the patchwork-painted junker.

She stood next to it, in stark contrast to the dull vehicle. The bright morning sun lit up her white uniform so that it seemed to glow, and the smudged hospital window blurred her into an angel. She looked pure and perfect, in a parking lot full of decaying vehicles owned by dying people.

She smoothed her dress and bent down to check her makeup in the side-view mirror. He gazed at her as she bent forward, and he wished for a telescope. *That wouldn't go over well in here.* He watched her until she walked out of view into the hospital entrance, and he was happy she appeared to be unmolested.

The door opened, and Dr. Mason entered the exam room. "How's it hanging, Borata?" he asked.

Tommy turned from the window and climbed up to sit on the strip of white paper on the exam bench. "I guess that's what I'm here to find out," he said. "How did the pictures come out?"

The doctor flipped through images on his computer screen, leaning forward occasionally for a closer look.

Tommy waited, staring out the window. Wanting to be free, wanting to be young again, wanting to be well, wanting to be anywhere but in a doctor's office.

Dr. Mason rose and went through the usual exam procedure: heart rate, breathe deep, breathe normal. He lifted Tommy's hands to examine his nails and noted the scrapes, scratches, and bruises. "What the hell have you been up to, Tommy?" he asked.

"Eh, me and Moses, you know, the black dude in treatment with me, we ah...we were working on his car, trying to get it running again."

The doctor raised an eyebrow over the top of his charts and grunted his skepticism. "Anyway. Seems like things have gone well with your treatment," Mason said. "The chemo and trial drugs have destroyed the tumors. There is no cure, you know that. But I think you're going to be okay for a while."

Tommy turned in disbelief. "No chemo today?"

"No, let's let you recover some, give it a little time, and check on things in a month or so."

"You sure?" Tommy asked.

"Yeah, I know," the doctor said. "You're feeling a bit happy, but a lot guilty? Afraid to accept it? That's all normal. Enjoy it. Go with it, Tommy. I've already notified the unit to cancel your treatment today."

Tommy went to the cafeteria and sat down with a fresh cup of coffee. It was good news, but he'd looked forward to his session with the others, and especially Nurse Carmen. He was happy about the prognosis but worried about telling Moses and how it might affect the bond between the two of them. When the time arrived for his treatment, he decided to go upstairs anyway.

"You're canceled, and you came anyway due to your love and desire for me, Chief?" Nurse Beulah asked as he entered the pod area.

"Nah, and nah," Tommy responded. "I'm gonna hang out with the gang. What the hell else do I have to do?"

"Suit yourself, just don't get everyone riled up."

Tommy sat back in his usual pod, closed his eyes, and let the good news soak in. He drifted between consciousness and sleep, letting the familiar sounds of the place wash over him.

"You're losing your touch, letting a black man sneak up on you like this."

Tommy jumped in his seat, startled to see Moses looming over him and wearing a satisfied smile. Eddie and Helen were there also, getting prepped for treatment by Beulah. Helen's husband Herb was by her side, as always.

"Yeah, kind of lost in thought I guess. Have a seat, partner." Tommy pulled the bag he'd been carrying around out from under his seat. "Here Mos, I brought you something."

Moses took the bag and removed a retro-style blue New York Rangers hat with red and white trim. "Aw, damn Chief, it ain't even Christmas, and here you come with presents," he said. "Rangers, huh? Black people gonna think I was Army Special Forces or something."

Tommy laughed. "Right. Not that kind of Rangers, but most people know the difference. You're a tough guy either way. Lace up the skates, they could use an enforcer this year."

Moses fished a nail clipper from his pocket and took his time removing the tags. He curved the bill of the hat with his big hands, then finally, he placed it on his head. "Damn, fitted cap, and it's just right. How'd you know my size?"

"I told the guy it was for someone with the biggest damn head I ever saw," Tommy said. The group all laughed together.

He nudged Moses while turning up the pod television. "Here's our guy again, let's see what's new."

A newscaster was beginning an update on the priest story. "...the priest, now identified as Father Damien Tarat, has confessed to the crimes and is being held..."

"Yes!" Tommy exclaimed, punching Moses on the arm. "Now he'll get his."

"Damn right," Moses replied. "One thing they don't like in the joint is child molesters. He's in for a rough ride."

Tommy thought about the good news from the doctor, and now from the newscaster. "It's a damn good day..." and didn't finish his thought as he looked around at the others.

"It's okay, brother," Moses said, picking up on his friend's regret. "We have to enjoy every little victory."

Nurse Carmen came into the room. "How's it going, kid?" Tommy asked her, changing the subject in the room.

"Oh, alright," she answered. "Everything is a bit crazy at home. Buster was out looking for work the other day and saw some woman getting mugged. He jumped into the middle and got all beat up. He's a damn mess, so I'm taking care of him now too. Then he gets a flat tire on top of everything. No good deed goes unpunished!"

Tommy and Moses looked at each other over the top of her back as she bent down to adjust the infusion stand, and shook their heads in disgust.

"Damn," Moses said. "A real hero."

Carmen straightened, and Tommy looked for any signs of bruising on her. "I have to say so. There's been a change in him lately. He's much mellower and nicer around the house. Must be getting old," she laughed.

Tommy feigned resentment. "And what's wrong with getting old?"

"Not a damn thing, Tommy. Beats the alternative, right?"

Carmen started to move away when Moses asked, "Ain't you going to hook up Tommy?"

She stopped and turned to face them. "Good news, Moses. Your buddy got a pass for a while. Seems like he might be in remission. I hear it has a lot to do with the nursing care at this place." She winked at them and walked away.

Moses reached out and gripped Tommy's shoulder. "Damn. That's great!"

Eddie perked up and offered his congratulations, and Helen said, "At least one of us is getting better."

Tommy could see Herb squeeze her frail, translucent hand. He heard the fear in her voice and saw it reflected in Herb's eyes, as well as Eddie's. He felt horrible for them, and guilty all over again. He knew they were all happy for him, but at the same time, they all wished it could've been them. "Thanks, guys. Eddie, where's the kid today?" he asked, trying to change the subject.

"Got school," Eddie answered. "Hey, what's wrong with both you guys' hands? Your knuckles are all busted up."

The busybody in Helen perked up, and she leaned forward to examine them as well.

Both men looked at their hands as if noticing the injuries for the first time. They spoke simultaneously to offer jumbled excuses about household maintenance and car repair.

"Looks to me like you fellas both got into a fight," Helen said.

Nurse Carmen was patrolling nearby and examined both of them. "Damn if she isn't right.

You boys been fighting each other, or beating up on your old ladies?" she asked.

Tommy kept his cop cool and laughed it off despite his concern she would correlate their injuries with her husband's. "Hell, if it was me and him going at it, I probably wouldn't be sitting here right now," he said, jerking his head at Moses.

The group gave a nervous laugh, and Moses nodded his head. "That's right."

Tommy continued. "We're both man's men, not some doctors with dainty hands. We were working on getting Moses' car up and running."

"Oh, when did you pick up a car, Mos?" Carmen asked.

Moses looked at Tommy. "Ah, picked it up from a neighbor, needs a lot of work…"

Helen and Eddie both looked at him with suspicion.

Tommy changed the subject. "Well, you fools aren't getting rid of me that easy. We all know how it goes; this is just a timeout, and I'll be back in the chair after a while. Besides, we're like a family here, so I'm not going anywhere. Even if I have to start putting on one of those white dresses and taking care of your butts myself."

"Now that I'd like to see," Beulah said as she passed by close enough to hear the comment.

They all went about their business. Tommy looked over at Moses, who was slumped in his seat, his eyes downcast.

He noticed Tommy's gaze and offered a false smile and a thumbs-up. "You got this licked, my brother."

"Thanks for the vote of confidence," Tommy replied. "I know the drill, though. My old man went through it years ago. Medicine wasn't then what it is now, but it still seems to be the same old cycle. You get notified, panic, get sicker, go through this shit." He waved at the equipment surrounding them.

"Then you get this 'remission, ' and everyone gets all happy and full of false hope. It's like the disease almost has a heart. It gives you that last happy, almost-normal time, an oasis in the middle of it all, then it comes back with a vengeance to claim its prize."

Moses looked down at his shoes. "Already done used up my oasis," he said.

Tommy realized he'd let his thoughts run away with him, without considering the effect of his words on the others. They looked demoralized.

"Ah shit, that's just me being a ray of sunshine as always. Good news is, the cure is coming soon for us. They're making progress, I've seen it in the news."

They smiled and nodded to each other in agreement.

It became quiet as the room moved in its usual symbiotic pace. His friends in the unit all looked older and sicker. Tommy watched them all sleep as the machines ticked and dispensed poisons into them. Moses snored lightly next to him. Emotions swirled through his mind and body. He became angry that good people had to endure this punishment, while the evil ones in the world seemed to be too often rewarded.

Overcome with sadness, he got up to leave. "I gotta go. Have a happy Thanksgiving everyone," he whispered to them.

Carmen and Beulah were tending to other patients and didn't see him pass through the door alone.

~*~

Margie reached out with a shaky hand and pulled her glass closer. When she let go, it continued to slide toward her on the wet kitchen table. "Come to Momma," she said with a laugh.

"You better give it a rest. You're past your usual limit, and you gotta drive home."

"Shut up, Diane. You're my sister, not my mother. And I'm a functional drunk, you know." She glanced over and saw that the words had stung, and regretted them. "I'm sorry, sis. Too much stress lately. I love you, you know that."

"So, I thought you were leaving him?"

"That was the plan," Margie said. "Now he's sick, how can I do that?"

Diane poured herself another half-glass of scotch. "Might as well ride it out, I guess. How long are they giving him?"

Margie twisted the tumbler as she spoke. "You know, the usual. A few years I guess. They just told him he's in remission, so who knows. Knowing that tough old bastard, he'll outlive me."

She drained her glass as her sister got up and walked into the bathroom. After hearing the door shut, she reached over and poured a small splash of scotch into her glass. She began to replace the bottle and then added to her drink. *One for the road.*

She thought about the past. She remembered being in love, optimistic about the future, seemingly without a problem in the world. With a rugged husband and delightful, happy little boy. There seemed to be two lives—that one, and the other which came out of nowhere and presented a starkly contrasting darkness. And then a reprieve; happiness returned again for a while in the form of forbidden love, before abruptly departing, giving way again to darkness.

She heard the toilet flush and threw the contents of the glass down her throat.

"What are you guys doing for Thanksgiving?" Diane asked.

"The usual. I guess it's a break from the monotony of life, but I do enjoy cooking the meal. Might as well enjoy it; it won't be long before Bobby moves out…and Tommy is gone. Then maybe I'll be eating here."

"You're always welcome, sister."

They heard the front door open. "Is that you, Jack?" Diane asked.

"In the flesh." Diane's husband entered and gripped her in a prolonged embrace. They began kissing demonstratively.

Margie cleared her throat. "Jesus, get a room." Jack looked over Diane's shoulder and winked at her.

Diane turned to her. "Can't anyone be in love? Try it sometime, sis."

Margie got up. "My turn to hit the little ladies' room. This stuff goes right through you."

"Um, use the upstairs one, please," her sister asked. "My stomach was upset if you catch my drift."

"Well, that sure kills the mood," Jack said.

Margie climbed the stairs and paused outside the hall bathroom. She reconsidered and entered the master bedroom instead, then shut the *en-suite* bathroom door behind her. She looked at herself in the mirror. *Old, ugly, fat.* She pulled back on the skin of her face with both hands to remove the wrinkles, and for a moment saw the young Margie from so long ago. She lost her grip, and the mask of reality returned.

She opened the medicine cabinet and selected a pill bottle. Holding it up to the light to read the label, she murmured her approval, and then opened it and took one. *Mmmm.* A bottle of cologne caught her eye. She opened it, closed her eyes, and waved it beneath her nose.

She allowed herself to drift back in time, the familiar fragrance transporting her. It opened a tunnel of memories, and scenes that were long past paraded through her mind.

She leaned back too far in her enjoyment of it and lost her balance, crashing backward into the towel rack. She grabbed it for balance, ripping it off the wall as she fell to the floor. The cologne splashed on her as she maintained her grip on it.

"What the hell, are you okay up there?" she heard her sister shout.

"I'm good, I'm good, no worries, be down in a minute."

She scrambled to her feet and replaced the cologne, then flushed the toilet and hurried out of the room and back down the stairs. Grabbing her purse and coat from the rack by the door, she shouted to her sister, "I've got to go, sorry. I love you," and went through the door.

11 THANKSGIVING

TOMMY TOOK IN THE SCENE in his home and reflected on how fortunate he was. Margie was bustling in the kitchen, singing to herself for the first time in a long time. He drew in long, deep breaths of aromatic turkey and thought about how nice it was to be able to think about food without vomiting. The Giants were on TV and winning for a change. Bobby was dozing in the recliner with a blanket over him, a full beer on his tray table.

Tommy reached for his glass of iced tea, dotted with beads of sweat, and drank half down in a single chug. He let the taste linger in his mouth, thankful he could taste again, eat again, drink again. He wondered what the other patients were doing, and hoped they weren't too sick from treatment to enjoy their Thanksgiving meal.

"Hey, lightweight. You going to drink that thing?" he asked his sleeping son.

Bobby rustled and rolled on his side, facing his dad, who he knew would persist if he didn't answer him. He yawned and reached for the beer, then checked the TV for the score. "Damn, Giants are winning."

"Yup. God bless America," Tommy responded.

Bobby pulled the lever on the side of the recliner and sat up, stretching. "How're you feeling, Pop?"

"Aces. Can't wait to eat." He turned toward the kitchen. "Margie, it's halftime. You need help?" She declined, and he turned back to his son.

"What's new? You been following the news? That shit with the priest? You working it at all?"

"Father Tarat?" Bobby answered. "Yeah, we're investigating it. There's a lot of people on it, including the Feds."

"Same old bullshit. The church covers it up, pays off the families out of its big fucking treasure chest." Tommy's voice rose with his anger. "Then they move these sick bastards somewhere else to do it again."

"Best keep it down. You don't want to piss off Mom with another one of your anti-Church rants. Keep it calm for dinner at least, okay?" Bobby asked.

"That's it, that's what feeds it all," Tommy said. "People afraid to deal with it, sweep it under the rug, pretend it isn't happening. I should've specialized in busting these creeps instead of dealing with the punks on the street. How would you feel if you were one of those kids he abused? Or if it was your kid?"

Bobby readjusted his blanket. "I'm sure it sucks. I hate it too. The whole church thing was always creepy to me. You guys made me go against my will, remember?"

"Yeah, *when* you went, that is," Tommy said. "I remember we caught you using the collection money we gave you to buy hot dogs to cook in the woods instead."

Bobby laughed. "I got away with it for a long time. You always asked me what color robes the priest was wearing, thinking you were keeping me honest. I knew damn well you had no idea since you always bragged that you only went to church for weddings and funerals."

"You ever think about getting out from behind the desk and getting involved in some of this stuff?" Tommy asked.

"Dad, we talked about this...I told you. I *am* involved with *some of this stuff*. I'm not a fucking secretary..."

"Watch the language in there, boys," came Margie's melodic warning.

Bobby continued. "It's all different now. Not all police work happens on the street. I'm doing my part like you did. I'm tracking things from my end—Internet traffic, things like that. Maybe someday you'll understand and be proud."

"I'm always proud, son..." Tommy replied.

"I think we're all set, boys, come on over and let's eat," Margie called from the dining room. They both got up and moved to their spots at the table.

Margie asked them whether either wanted to say the words. She paused a moment, got the lack of response she expected, and moved on while they all bowed their heads.

When she finished, Tommy spoke up. "And please Lord, look over my fellow patients in the Big C unit, after the souls of my parents, and my friend and partner Paulie. Amen."

"Oh!" Margie exclaimed in shock. Bobby was also taken aback and looked at his father.

"Just adding in a few words for those we lost," Tommy said. "Let's eat." He eyed Margie as she filled her large water glass from the magnum of wine. She didn't return his gaze.

They passed serving dishes, piled their plates high, and ate to the melody of silverware sounding on china.

"How's other things?" Tommy asked his son. "You got your eye on anyone special yet?"

"Don't even go there," Bobby answered.

"Tommy, you know to leave him alone about that. Everything in its own time," Margie gently scolded him.

Tommy was feeling playful, on top of his growing angst about his son growing older and living at home without anyone else in his life. "C'mon, kid. What, she's black? Jewish? It's okay. Everyone's welcome here. Bring her over, we can handle it. I'm a changed man, you know."

Bobby slammed his bottle of beer down to the table with a loud clunk, and it spewed foam from the top like a grade-school volcano project. "Really?" he asked. His expression was taut.

"Please! Don't spoil the day!" Margie begged.

"Okay, okay, new subject. Jesus," Tommy said, and went back to eating. Margie rose and dutifully mopped up the beer, and then grabbed the magnum and refilled her glass.

They discussed less dramatic topics, sprinkled with compliments about the meal. Margie had gone quiet after a while, and Tommy looked over at her.

She quickly wiped her cheek and scraped back her chair. "I'm going to get dessert ready," she said.

"You okay?" Tommy asked her.

"Yes. Damn onions get me every time," she answered, unconvincingly.

"C'mon, kid," Tommy said to Bobby, "Let's clear the table while she's doing that."

After clearing the dishes, they sat at the dining room table for coffee. Margie was quiet and withdrawn. Bobby fiddled with his phone.

"It's still early. How would you two like to go somewhere with me?" Tommy asked.

Bobby looked up. "Where to?"

"A friend from the hospital asked for help. He gives out meals over at the shelter every turkey day. He asked if anyone who might have time could stop by to help out."

"I have to meet friends later for a few beers," Bobby answered. "But I can go for a while."

"You fellas go ahead," Margie said. "I'm going to put on a movie and relax."

~*~

As they neared their destination, Bobby broke the silence in the car. "Wow, I didn't ever think I'd see you in this part of town unless you were working."

"Things change, son. People change. I'm learning more now than I ever did on the force. Back then I was only getting one point of view, blinded by the machismo of the job and the people I was working with. I'm seeing things different now that I'm on the outside."

Bobby put his hand on his father's shoulder. "That's great, Dad. I'm proud of you. Maybe there is hope for civilization."

They both laughed as Tommy parked the car. They got out and entered the shelter, which was warm and smelled of good food. The mood was bright and happy, despite the obvious dire straits most of the occupants were in. People were eating at long rows of folding tables, smiling.

"This way," Tommy said. He walked to the front of the hall, where Moses was scooping food from industrial-sized pots onto the plates of a long line of eager customers.

He greeted his busy friend, who hadn't noticed their approach. "Well, if it ain't Chef Boyardee," Tommy yelled above the din. "This here's my boy, Bobby."

Moses smiled and shook Bobby's hand. "Must've been a tough tour growing up under the General here," he said to Bobby.

"You have no idea," Bobby replied.

"Slap on a couple of aprons, fellas, and get busy back here serving our customers."

They spent time spooning food onto the plates of grateful, hungry citizens. It energized Tommy to help the needy families. *Citizens. They're citizens. I used to look down at them as trash, and a nuisance. As lazy and entitled, when they were suffering.*

Throughout the evening, they rotated through different responsibilities. Tommy found himself busing tables and took time to engage the diners. He noticed Moses and Bobby ducking out for a break as the crowd thinned inside the shelter. *Good, maybe Mos can get through to him.*

Tommy sat with a family in holiday attire and asked the children what they wanted for Christmas.

"Just some nice sneakers," said the young boy.

"A new dress for school," said his sister. "And maybe some candy," she added after a pause.

That son-of-a-bitch priest, molesting beautiful kids like this for all these years. He suppressed his anger, picked up their trays, and looked to see if Bobby had come back in. "You folks have a good evening. Be careful going home." He stopped at the next table to sit with an elderly man who was eating alone. "How you doing tonight, pal? Can I get you anything else?" he asked.

"No, sir," the man replied. He looked at Tommy and then back at his plate.

"How're doing? Okay?" He waited, but the man didn't answer. He placed a hand on the man's shoulder and got up, and then thought he heard him say something.

"What's that, pal?" he asked.

Tommy sat back down. The man spoke louder but continued to look at his plate. "I know you. I remember you. You and your partner, riding around our block all the time. You both was hell on us. We wasn't doing nothing, and you was still hell on us, all the time."

"Yeah, hey, I'm sorry. I wasn't a good person. I'm trying to make up for it. I'm sick now. Doing things like this, it makes me realize…"

"Now you sick, and you come in here for a night serving food, trying to atone before you go for judgment?" the man asked. "I'm not so sure it works like that, *pal*."

"No, no, uh, I'm doing a lot more," Tommy said. "Trying to do more. I understand now. I see things better."

"People who are well off are always looking down at us. Saying shit like, 'In this country, anybody can make it, so why you lazy people don't want to work? You should've studied in school. School is free, you didn't learn.' You motherfuckers all had perfect TV-Land families. Mom and dad helping with the homework and going to back-to-school night. Don't know how it is for a kid to grow up in a tenement, no heat, drugged-out, abusive parents if they even had any. Schools without damn pencils and paper, teachers who don't give a rat's ass."

Tommy listened intently and had contempt for the man he used to be. For the first time, he saw the plight of the unfortunate through a clear lens. "I understand now. All I can say to you is that I'm sorry. I'm really so sorry."

"That'll have to be good enough," the man said. "Thank you for doing what you're doing here tonight." The man looked up from his plate for the first time and engaged Tommy eye-to-eye. "I forgive you," he said with a tired smile.

Tommy rose to leave, and the man rose with him. They embraced, and Tommy felt the warmth of the man's body through the softness of his timeworn clothing.

~*~

Bobby and Moses made their way up a flight of stairs to the rooftop landing.

Moses reached into his pocket and withdrew a metal cigarette case. He snapped it open and took out a joint. Replacing the case, he fished out a lighter and lit it, drawing deep.

"Care to partake?" he asked Bobby.

"Nah, drug testing and all. You know the deal," Bobby responded. "Smells damn good though."

They both leaned back against the brick wall of the shelter, bracing against the cold, enjoying the quiet and the star-speckled sky above them.

"Seems like your pop in there is enjoying himself."

"Yeah, he's all into this Good Samaritan thing now. It's good to see him doing stuff like this. He's different now that he's sick."

"I like your old man, kid," Moses said.

The quiet returned as Moses consumed his smoke and they both stared into the night.

"I'm gay," Bobby said.

"I'm Moses." They both laughed at the exchange. "It's not a big deal these days. Why you telling me this, kid?" Moses asked him.

Bobby shifted uncomfortably. "I don't know. Practicing, I guess."

"For the main event, right inside there?" Moses asked.

"Yeah, I suppose. You know any gay people?"

"Bobby, I been to prison. Everybody gay in prison, at least for a little while. Whether they like it or not." They both laughed again. "Times are different now," Moses continued. "Most folks don't give a rat's ass what you do on your own time, long as nobody's getting hurt. Be yourself. Your old man's still gonna love you. He's different now."

"It's hard to imagine. I've been hiding this so long. I can't imagine that 'guess who's coming to dinner' moment with my family."

"Move away, maybe. Makes things easier sometimes, to be your own person."

"Yeah, that's not a half-bad idea, Moses. But I don't know if I can handle living as a gay person anywhere. Things are better, but society is still a pretty cruel place."

The wind picked up, and Moses zipped up his jacket. "You want to go back in?"

Bobby didn't answer for a while, and Moses waited patiently.

"You heard about that priest thing?" Bobby asked him.

The question brought Moses a moment of alarm, before he decided to feel him out. "Yeah, I've seen some of that in the news. Hope he gets what he's got coming. I trust in you cops to take care of that business and put him away."

Bobby became animated and pushed away from the wall, suddenly angry. "Fuck the cops, that motherfucker needs to die for what he's done." He walked to the edge of the rooftop and paused.

His sudden change in demeanor took Moses by surprise. For a moment he thought Bobby might jump, and began to move toward him. "Hey, let's get on inside. Getting cold up here."

Bobby spun and walked past him. "Yeah, it's cold."

~*~

Tommy stared up at the ceiling as Margie adjusted her pillow and read her magazine, both of them lying in bed. He reached for the remote and turned on the television, flipping through channels, pausing at each to determine content or wait through commercials. He lingered on a Spanish-language channel showing a *telenovela*. The starlet reminded him of Carmen, and he became aroused as he watched her male costar seduce her and remove her evening gown.

"What the hell are you doing?" Margie demanded.

He realized he'd moved his hand to her leg under the covers, and quickly removed it while sitting up to hide his erection. "I'm learning Spanish."

He flipped the channel to sports, and she shook her head and went back to her reading.

After a period of awkward silence, Tommy broke the ice. "You were upset at dinner. Everything okay?"

She answered without taking her gaze away from her reading. "Yes, it's fine. It was emotional when you talked about the people we lost—your dad, and Paulie."

"Yeah, it is emotional. I think about them every day," Tommy responded. "I wonder if they're here with us. Maybe in some kind of different dimension we can't detect. Maybe they come back as animals or something. Maybe that's why animals aren't allowed to communicate with us."

She ignored his musings and changed the subject. "And Bobby—leave him alone. He'll find his way. You have to give him time. He's doing okay. He's working, it's not like he's hanging out and doing drugs."

"I know it. Sometimes they need a little nudge though, you know? He's no kid anymore. What the hell's he going to do, live here with us the rest of his life? He needs a good woman like I got." He patted her thigh.

Margie put the magazine down and looked at him. "Don't patronize me. What if he doesn't want a girl?"

Tommy laughed. "Of course he does." His voice rose. "Of course he does. What the hell are you talking about?"

She knew to leave it at that and clicked off her reading light before changing the subject again.

"How did it go over there tonight? I worried enough about you being in that part of town when you were working; now you have to go back, with Bobby?"

"It was good. They're good people that need help. I never saw that before. I spent too much of my time hating people, prejudiced by my job. I'm seeing things different now. Besides, I got a lot of stuff to atone for. I'm looking for a pass at the Pearly Gates," he said. The humor had returned to his voice.

"Good Lord," she responded. "Try going to church and saying your prayers. Good night, Tommy."

"Good night, honey," he replied. He gave her the usual peck and then puffed his pillow and rolled over to his normal position, facing away from her. He set the TV sleep timer to sixty minutes, to prevent the awkward silence that exposed their lack of intimacy.

He lay awake, but with his eyes closed. He could sense the flickering screen. His thoughts went to what had just happened. He was embarrassed and guilty about being in bed with his wife while thinking of another woman.

She's been there with me through everything. She's still here, devoted to me after so many years of my bullshit. Who the hell would stick it out through that? She never complained. She worked her ass off, every day, at work and then here, to make a home for us. What is it about us that tempts us to throw everything we have away for a few minutes of pleasure? What a fucked-up species we are.

He changed channels to the evening news. He waited through the mundane stories to see if the priest had been sentenced yet. The anchor revealed that they had exclusive coverage—an interview with one of the victims. He looked over at Margie, who'd dozed off, and sat up in rapt attention.

The scene cut to an interviewer, seated across from a figure presented in shadow for anonymity—a clean silhouette, disrupted only by a stray cowlick. The interviewer spoke first.

"We're here with someone who says he was a victim of Father Damien Tarat's abuses from two decades ago. We have concealed his image and voice in order to protect his identity. Sir, my first question is, how did you come to know Father Tarat?"

The figure stirred, clearly uncomfortable, and then spoke in a robotic, computer-obfuscated voice. "He was my Scout leader. He was fun; the most popular one. He knew magic tricks. All the kids wanted his attention. I was shy, but he picked me. Maybe others. He said he'd teach me magic. He said we had to be alone because I was the only one he was going to teach…"

There was a pause while the subject tried to collect himself. The interviewer, not wanting to lose her scoop, said a few comforting words and offered to stop for a while.

The subject continued. "It all happened slow. A little at a time. He said it was normal. He said God wanted him to teach me about things, to teach me not to be so shy and uncomfortable with myself."

"Did you tell anyone?" the interviewer asked.

"No. I was a kid, and I was in denial about it. And I don't think I realized how bad it was, at least at first. I didn't think anyone would believe me, and I didn't want to be in trouble. I thought, if he's a priest, he must be doing the right thing. He kept saying that God was okay with it."

"We want to thank you for speaking out, and we're sorry that you were a victim…"

"I'm still a victim. I'll always be a victim," the subject interjected.

"Understood, and hopefully Father Tarat never hurts another soul."

As the programming went to commercial, Tommy started to rouse from his silent observation. As he watched, something had stirred in him, well beneath the surface—some vague sense of familiarity and disbelief. He pushed it away and let it be replaced by an anger that boiled up from within him. "Dirty scumbag!" he shouted.

"Turn it off, please," Margie said from the depths of her pillow.

He turned the television off, scooted over to her, and put his arm around her. In that simple act, and the sudden warmth of their bodies together, he found the long-lost comfort of the many years they'd once slept that way. His anger transformed to tears and deep sighs of sadness, which he tried to hide from his wife.

She stirred, and mumbled, "What's wrong?"

"I love you, Margie. That's all. I just want you to know I love you."

She responded in kind, muffled by the pillow, and took his hand.

I have to let this go. He'll rot in prison, that's good enough for me… Did she say she loves me or loved *me?*

12 A PLAN

LUCIUS STOOD VIGIL behind the bar at Wyla's, wearing his sunglasses and headphones. Moses sat bent over on his stool next to Tommy. The tavern was dark, with few patrons. Blues music flowed through the jukebox, featuring a mournful blues harp solo, and a TV flickered above the bar. Ancient multicolored holiday lights were strung up along the ceiling, the working ones blinking in ragged unison. A synthetic Christmas tree stood in one corner, sparsely appointed with ornaments. Tommy was accepted now, out of respect for Moses, and perhaps as a shield against the police.

Moses threw back a shot and chased it with his beer. He spoke while looking down at the grimy bar. "We done the right thing with Vela, right? It's still bugging me. I don't want to get busted again."

Tommy turned to him. "C'mon man. It's done. You have to admit, it felt good to fix that problem and give him what he deserved. That's the best I felt in a long time. We should do more like that. We're dying, Mos. Fucking dying. Why not do more like that, to atone for the things we both have on our conscience? What are they going to do, put us in jail?"

"You're getting better, Tommy. You got this beat. I'm too far down the road. I'm thinking maybe I just want to run this out quietly."

"Fuck that. This remission is a respite for me, and you know it. We're on borrowed time, both of us. And you're Moses fucking Taylor. A legend. My partner in crime."

They both laughed, and the laughing inspired a round of tired coughs and hacks from Moses.

"You see that guy on TV last night?" Tommy asked. "The one molested by the priest when he was a kid?"

"I did," Moses responded, pausing and looking at him with some apprehension. "He'll get his in prison, like I said. He better bring the lube and be careful not to drop the soap in the community shower."

Tommy looked up at the television as the evening news began, and signaled to Lucius, who nodded and flipped switches to mute the jukebox and turn up the TV.

A news reporter stood in front of a church as snow flurried around her, whipping her hair against her face.

"...We have shocking breaking news in the story of Father Tarat..."

"Jesus, what now?" Tommy asked.

"...the guilty verdict against Father Tarat has been vacated. An appellate court has ruled that Tarat's confession, in which he described himself as a homosexual, may have caused jurors to create in their minds an unfounded association between homosexuality and pedophilia..."

"Motherfucker!" Tommy jumped from his bar stool and paced the checkered floor. "The motherfucker is out!" He swung wildly with his fists, and then stopped and returned to his seat. "Mos, we have to do something. I want to get that son of a bitch."

The reporter continued, "Tarat's whereabouts are unknown. The diocese has not offered any comment, other to say they will ensure that Tarat will be reassigned and will have no contact with children."

Tommy sat in stunned disbelief. Moses stirred. "Only the scum of the earth does what he did...what he's been doing."

"Yeah," Tommy responded in a whisper, full of resolve. "That's exactly what I've been talking about. I'd feel good about delivering justice to him. The perfect case. He's guilty, but now he won't be held accountable. Just thinking about all the kids he hurt makes my blood boil.

"One thing eats away at me. A long time ago, I pulled a priest over for speeding. He had a kid in the car, kid looked scared. I asked the kid if he was okay, but he never got a chance to answer. The priest said the kid had a troubled past: parents in and out of jail, reform school, probation, and was terrified of cops. I bought it and let him go. Can't give a priest a ticket, right? Jesus. Maybe that was this guy. Maybe I could've stopped this a long time ago." He thought about it for a while, becoming angrier at himself. "You want to do it?"

"What, like Vela?" Moses asked.

"No. I'm talking about taking him out. Fuck it. We'll be vigilantes for justice. Like superheroes. Closest we'll ever get. We're dying. Let's do the world a favor on the way out. I got shit to atone for."

"Oh man. That's a whole different level than what we did with Vela," Moses replied.

Tommy grabbed his friend's arm. Lucius took note from across the room and stirred. "*He* is on a whole different level than Vela. How many kids do you think this scumbag fucked up for the rest of their lives, Mos? Imagine if it was your kid."

"I don't know about this," Moses said. "Can you do it, kill someone? You ever killed anyone?

"C'mon. I've been to Nam. I was a cop in the city for thirty years. What about you?"

Moses hesitated. "I didn't mean it. I was drunk, and I did my time for it. I do my penance every day for it. The question is, could you do it again, Tommy?"

"This time I feel justified. He needs to go. I'll do it for those kids, and never feel bad."

"I don't know if I could do it. I might choke," Moses responded.

"That's on me. I want him. You're just the help."

Moses leaned back and looked at him. "Excuse me?"

Tommy suppressed the urge to laugh. "Alright, alright. Listen. Let me come up with a plan. I'll get the 4-1-1 on him and come up with something. Hear me out, and then we can make a decision."

"And what if someone finds out and rats us out before we can do anything? You'll get a slap on the wrist, being an ex-cop, and I'll spend my last miserable days in jail."

"Moses, this and anything like this we discuss stays between us. It's the only way. We agreed, it's our code. Otherwise, we'll go down together. Right?"

Moses hesitated. "That's right. Who the hell am I going to talk to anyway? You do your plan and let's talk about it later. They said 'reassigned.' He's probably in Idaho or somewhere by now."

"I bet he hasn't left yet," Tommy said. "But time is wasting."

13 SURVEILLANCE

MOSES WATCHED THE CHURCH rectory building through the windshield. "Damn, it's cold, Chief." As he spoke, white clouds rushed from his lips. "Turn the damn engine on so we can get some heat in here."

"Can't, Mos. Surveillance 101. If he's in there, he's probably looking out every five minutes. If he sees the exhaust, he'll know he's being watched. Let's wait a little longer, then we'll scram."

"I don't think he's there. It'd be stupid. The place has been dark all night, not a single light. How's he gonna be in there? It's the most obvious place he could be. He's not that dumb."

"In all my experience, surprisingly, people do exactly that. They stick with where they're comfortable, despite the odds. Sometimes they figure it's the last place people will look. Let's give it a little more time."

"How could he be sitting in there in the dark?"

"He probably has the windows blacked out. He'll screw up sooner or later. Then at least we'll know where he is, and we can keep an eye on him until he tries to leave."

Tommy was determined to wait for that one mistake. His stubbornness prevailed over his sympathy for his sick friend.

Moses shifted uncomfortably. "Before my old man died, he told me he saw stuff when he was working in that church that made him uncomfortable." He began another round of coughing, and then opened the passenger door and leaned out to vomit. When the attack had finally passed, he closed the door gently and wiped his mouth with his coat sleeve.

Tough bastard. I have to get him out of here, Tommy thought. He noticed the slightest flicker of light in one of the rectory windows. "Mos…look."

The side entrance opened, and a dark figure carrying a bag slid out. The person moved quickly to a nearby dumpster and raised the lid. He deposited the bag and closed the lid gently, and in a moment was back inside the building.

"Damn," Moses said. "Busted because he couldn't stand the smell of his trash anymore."

"You got it, brother. Now you're getting good at this. We have to figure out how to get that trash bag and go through it to see what we can learn. It's too risky to go over there."

"I got this. This one I know how to handle. Let me do it and then let's get the hell out of here." Moses opened the passenger door again. This time he ducked out and ran in a crouch to the supermarket on their side of the street. He paused next to the building, pulled the hood of his jacket up over his head, and tied it under his chin. He loosened his belt, so his pants hung down low, and then pulled his shirt tail out, so it hung sloppily over them.

Next, he pulled a shopping cart from the rack and wheeled it over to the supermarket's dumpster. He began picking out cans and bottles, depositing them in the cart. He wheeled the cart down the street on their side for a block, and then crossed and walked back toward the church. He stopped at public wastebaskets and sifted through the contents for more recyclables, slowly working his way down the street. When he reached the church parking lot, he opened the dumpster, removed the bag of trash and put it in his cart.

Tommy watched in amazement. *Son of a gun, he's good. Why didn't I think of that?*

Moses continued his routine past the church. He turned and signaled Tommy to go down the street to rendezvous. Tommy started the car, pulled around the block away from the church, and moved down the street to where Moses was heading.

Moses approached the car and grabbed the trash bag from the cart. He pulled the rear passenger door open and heaved the bag in, then jumped into the front. As they moved down the road and the car's heater kicked in, the stench of their cargo became more apparent. "God damn, what the hell's that man been eating?" Moses exclaimed.

Tommy pulled the car over. "Jesus. Put that shit in the trunk, will you Mos?" He pulled the trunk release lever, and Moses jumped out to take care of the problem.

Tommy heard the trunk slam, and a police cruiser pulled up behind them and activated its light bar. An officer climbed out and shouted to Moses, "Hold right there, sir." Moses placed his hands on the trunk and assumed a spread-eagled position.

Tommy emerged from the driver's side. The officer recognized him immediately. "Borata, what the hell are you doing out here? What's this, are you guys Nick Nolte and Eddie Murphy in *48 Hours*?"

Tommy approached and gripped the officer's hand. He did his best to deflect, hoping the cop hadn't seen too much. "Rogers, shouldn't you be back there in the coffee shop eating donuts? What're *you* doing out here?"

"I'm on patrol. You know the deal. There's been a lot of death threats on the priest in that church back there. *If* he's in there. I'm sure you heard what's going on with that son of a bitch. Still, we have to keep an eye on the place, so it's not vandalized or whatever. Maybe not too closely, if you know what I mean."

They shared a laugh, and Tommy responded, "Yeah, I hear you. No lower scum than scum like that. I'm sure you guys will do your job, and he'll get what he has coming when he goes to meet his maker."

"Uh, hello," Moses said, still spread-eagled against the car.

"Stand down, sir," Rogers said. He looked back at Tommy. "So, ah, back to my question, Borata. What's up?"

"This is my buddy, Moses." The two shook hands. "He's a fellow cancer patient, and we do treatment together, along with some other poor bastards." He considered whether Rogers had seen the shopping-cart drill. "He's down on his luck. I'm giving him a lift."

Rogers looked skeptical and was about to continue his line of questioning, but Tommy jumped in before he could. "Hey, Rogers. I'm running late getting home and need to run Mos to his place. The old lady gets cranky when I'm out late, starts thinking I'm playing the field. Can you imagine that?"

Rogers laughed. "No, not you. You're the only straight arrow I know, Borata, even though you do your share of window-shopping. Alright. I do need a cup of joe, and it isn't getting any warmer out here. Drive safely. Nice meeting you, Moses."

Moses and Tommy got into the car and drove off. Moses broke the silence. "That shit scares me. I don't need anyone putting two and two together, Tommy."

"Relax, Mos. We're good. You heard the man. He didn't see shit. Besides, cops aren't going to be too quick to think hard about going after anyone who takes out a piece of shit like that."

"My damn heart is going a mile a minute. I'm gonna have a stroke hanging out with you before this cancer finishes me off."

"Well, you aren't sitting home sick and bored," Tommy laughed. He pulled up in front of Moses' apartment building. "I'm going to find somewhere to go through this trash real quick. I'll let you know what I find tomorrow."

"I think you're going to find some damn smelly trash. Hold your nose. Alright. Sweet dreams, whitey." Moses exited the car, climbing up his stoop and into the complex.

When Tommy arrived home, he pulled into the garage and quickly went through the garbage. He stashed a few items of interest away to check out later and put the rest of it into the trash can. He entered the house, changed and cleaned up in the bathroom, and tried to get into bed with Margie as stealthily as possible.

She stirred and asked, "How was your card game, honey?"

"It was fine, Margie. Big winner tonight. Let's get some sleep and talk in the morning. I love you."

"You smell like garbage."

"Thanks, honey."

14 CEMETERY

WHILE HE WAITED FOR MOSES to arrive, Tommy read the words on the speckled gray headstone aloud. "Paul Edward Campagna." The small chips of quartz in the granite reflected the sunlight. *Paulie, my mentor. Paulie, my pseudo-big brother. Always one year older, one year wiser, one step ahead.*

Tommy squatted, trying to reconcile the contents of the earth beneath him with the friend who had shared most of his life. Memories flashed through his mind, one after another, like choppy 8mm home-movie clips: Paulie, his hero, scoring on the football field. Paulie, his hero, making out with the girls he could only fantasize about. Paulie, his hero, always there with big-brother advice and encouragement. Paulie, his hero, picture splashed across the front page of the newspaper under the headline: 'Cop Slain in Bodega Heist.'

He looked across the cemetery. The sun had retreated behind an ominous cloud. The stark gray trees blended with the dull man-made colors of the grave markers, gravel roadway, and iron cemetery fence. He looked back to his friend's name on the headstone.

"How you doing, pal?" Tommy asked the silent monument. Tommy imagined what he would've said. While he composed his friend's response, he picked at the tip of a rock embedded in the ground.

I'm doing okay, Tommy. Don't worry about me; worry about yourself. I am where I am, and you're still in the world. Take care of yourself.

He pushed at the tip of the rock again with his finger.

"I know you're watching, maybe watching over me. I'm troubled, big buddy. I'm sick. Sick inside, sick of people, sick of the state of this society. It's worse since you left, getting worse all the time.

"I guess I got a bit of a pass with the Big C. They say I'm stabilized. For now, at least."

He tried to move the tip of the rock back and forth, but it wouldn't budge. His finger was starting to bleed, but he kept at it. The rock didn't belong there. It was the only part of the gray ugliness he felt he could control.

"I got a plan with this other guy—black fella, can you believe that? Good guy. We kind of thought this plan up on account of us both dying from cancer; maybe we'll clean this world up a bit before we check out, do some good. Something you would've loved, right out of the movies. But now I'm getting better, and he's getting worse. I'm worried about getting him in trouble. There's this priest—he's a bad guy, real bad. He needs to be dealt with. Hurt some kids. I don't know now…maybe it's not such a good idea. I'm conflicted, Paulie."

Do what sets you free, Tommy. Do what your heart tells you. You're good, you were always the good one. Soon we'll be together again. Everything is temporary, except here in the hereafter. Make me proud. You always made me proud.

A nearby disturbance caught his attention. Several young men were walking past the cemetery, outside the tall spike-tipped fence: white, black, mixed race, and Latino. *At least the kids are all getting along better these days, race-wise.*

He watched their cocky, arrogant swaggering. They wore their pants pulled down in the back, buttocks in boxer briefs proudly displayed, with long silver chains dangling from their belts. *How the hell do those pants stay up?*

The young men traded profane rap lyrics without regard for others in the area and playfully jostled one another. *Like young predatory animals, preparing for real combat later in their lives.*

They spotted Tommy squatting by the headstone. The leader of the group walked up to the fence to address him. "You picking out your new crib, old man?" The others laughed and pushed at one another, then stopped to wait for Tommy's response.

Tommy rose to his feet, cursing the effort it took these days, and cursing the punks for making him do it. "Keep moving and mind your own business."

The rest of them crowded up to the fence, holding onto the thin iron bars and pushing their faces through the space between them. "Don't make us come in there, motherfucker. You be moving in for good before you know it, grandpa," one of them said.

Animals in the zoo. But I'm the one in the cage. "Move along." Tommy pulled back his jacket to expose the concealed-carry weapon in his underarm holster.

The leader took a step back from the fence and pulled up his sweatshirt to expose an even larger firearm jutting from his waistband. Several of his companions did the same.

Fuck. Tommy took his gun out and assumed a firing stance, taking aim at the body mass of the leader. "You pull that out," Tommy said, "and you better know how to use it. Or you'll be the one moving into this house. I'll take you all down before you can blink. Try running from me in those baggy pants, you little bastards."

The leader held his ground. "Why we need to be running? You saying we're bad because we're nasty? Back in your day, old man, you all had your jeans so damn tight you couldn't sit down without busting your ass out, right?" His entourage laughed. "We all got our thing, Pops. Don't hate."

The youths shouted insults and threats to him. He tried to keep his focus, but his arms were getting tired, and his legs were beginning to ache. He inched toward a large monument to use it for cover and could hear them discussing whether to surround and rob him. *This would be a good time to have a cell phone to call 911 if I wasn't so stubborn about using the damn things...*

~*~

Moses reluctantly rose from the couch and shuffled to the thermostat on the wall of his apartment. He twisted the dial just slightly, calculating the effect of additional comfort on his monthly gas bill. *Cold. I'm always so cold now.*

As was his habit, he moved a few steps sideways to stand before a cluster of pictures on his wall. His eyes moved to his favorite, one of him and Angie standing together on their wedding day. The picture was as faded as his memory of it.

Summer day. The happiest day of our lives. Everything before us. Young and naïve. We didn't have much; didn't want much. We just wanted to be together every day. We took those words to heart that most people blindly recite—'for richer or poorer, sickness or health.'

He thought about how little they had, yet how happy they always seemed to be. How they took pleasure from the simple things they shared together: the morning coffee that started their day, how they walked together to her bus stop as she headed off to work and he continued the two miles to his factory job.

They each looked forward so much to the end of the day: having dinner together then lying in their simple bed talking about the day and their future, the radio playing softly. Eventually, they would fall asleep curled together, exhausted. When she was alive, and they were so much in love, he looked forward to each of those simple repetitions, and now that he was alone he felt enslaved by them.

It seemed to him that those years had gone too swiftly, although they'd cherished every day within them, truly in love. Not the short-lived love that most couples had, but enduring, lasting, forever love. They saved money where they could, went without simple pleasures, kept the heat low and dressed in layers, just so that someday they could realize their postponed dream of a honeymoon in Hawaii—a dream that never came to pass.

While his eyes stayed focused on the picture, his mind replayed scenes from the years and events that followed, further down the road for them, after the period of non-eventful bliss.

One night they'd been making love, and in his passion he gripped her firm breasts while she sat above him, grinding herself into him in ecstasy, and felt something different—something that didn't belong there.

He knew there was no way he could interrupt their passion to discuss it, nor would he interrupt the period of blissful peace that followed their lovemaking, as their sweat dissipated and their breathing returned to normal, and they held each other in silence. That was sacred, and he could not broach the topic to violate it.

Nor did he want to bring it up the following morning, because the ritual they followed was also sacred to them and should never be tarnished. He did not want to send her off to her day in the sewing shop alarmed and stressed. It could wait until dinner.

He then convinced himself that perhaps he was wrong, perhaps it was simply her rib, and rather than upset her, he would wait to check again and be more sure of his conclusion before sending her off to the doctor. He knew it would take convincing, as it always did with her, to get her to spend the money on herself for a doctor visit.

After a time, he pretended it didn't happen, forgot about it, and selfishly allowed their happy status quo to continue until the night she came out of the shower, naked and holding her breast, eyes wide in fear, saying "Moses, what do you think this is? Do you feel something here?"

And then the guilt that followed as she went down the path to the inevitable ending that they both knew was coming. He cursed himself at each of the appointments he accompanied her to. At each of the treatments, then at each of the hospital visits, then finally every day and every night as she lay in their bed, the one where he'd committed his only sin against her, moaning in agony until finally, she was silent.

Bringing himself back to the present, he moved to the kitchen and took his battery of prescriptions. *I'm coming, honey. It's all going to be alright. We'll be together, and the promised land will be our honeymoon, forever and ever. Just like we talked about.*

He looked up at the kitchen clock and saw that it was time to leave to meet Tommy. He pulled his coat from a hook and headed down the stairs, closing the door on the tomb of memories behind him.

Outside, he stopped to talk to Lukas and a few of the Black Eagles who were hanging around the stoop. "You best start getting these bikes ready for winter, boys. Talk to old Joe and ask him if you can store them up in the warehouse till spring," Moses said.

Lukas responded, "Not us, Uncle. We been talking. We're gonna try to ride right on through, except for the snow days. That's what real men do. It's damn cold, but sure beats walking."

"Suit yourself. I'm out of here, I got to meet Tommy over at the cemetery. I'll be back in a while. You fuckers stay outta trouble, you hear?" he asked.

"You know us, Uncle Mos. We're the good guys. No bullshit for us, just a 'lil weed for the head to stay steady, and we don't go looking for no trouble."

He started down the street, imagining her hand in his, heading to the bus stop, as he always did when walking this route. He imagined the way he would often stop and twirl her as if dancing, and how she always acted surprised and giggled as if it had happened for the very first time.

He reached the bus stop and paused. This was where they always kissed goodbye, long enough to draw attention and teasing from the neighbors who would cat-call and whistle at them and teasingly call him an owned man after she'd left. He thought about how he wore it with pride.

He remembered the day she told him she was pregnant and the joyful planning that followed.

The long list of names they could never make shorter or come to agreement on.

He thought about the day he received an emergency call at his job. It was from her employer, telling him she'd had an 'accident' and was in the hospital, and he went there and cried with her over losing the child.

He thought about how he'd almost convinced her to try again—before she found out about the lump. *I ain't leaving you to raise no child on your own, not without me, Moses Taylor.* He imagined the child, fully grown in his image. *Someone to carry on in my place.*

He thought about all the pain he and those he loved had suffered due to the hatred and prejudice they'd experienced all their lives, and wondered how he could stand seeing his child endure that. He wondered what he would've done if his precious child had been molested by Father Tarat. *I know what I would do.*

He rounded the final corner to the cemetery and began his descent down the hill leading to it. Below him, a scene unfolded—a man taking cover behind a large tomb, crouched in a firing stance. On the other side of the cemetery fence, a group of young men seemed to be taunting him menacingly. *Son of a bitch.*

He turned swiftly and began to retrace his steps as quickly as he could. Pain wracked his body as his abused joints and cancer-wracked torso endured a pace he hadn't attempted in a very long time, alternately limping and hopping with each step.

As he approached the block and saw the Eagles ahead, he attempted to shout to them, but the wheezing words could not reach their destination. Lukas saw him coming and jumped to his feet, prompting the rest of the Eagles to do the same. "What the fuck, Uncle Mos?"

Moses finally reached them. "Saddle the fuck up, we got trouble down the hill. That goddamn white guy has got himself into the shit with a bunch of punks."

"Uncle Mos, you know every time we get involved with the whites, it's gonna be us going to jail or some shit. I don't know…" Lukas replied.

"Saddle the fuck up, motherfuckers! That's an order, not a request. Let's go."

The men mounted their bikes and cranked the engines, blipping the throttles to warm the cold engines beyond the stall point. Moses hobbled to Lukas' bike and grabbed his pants leg to pull his leg over the seat. Lukas handed him a half-shell helmet, and he placed it haphazardly on his head, buckling the strap.

Lukas gave the signal, and the group peeled away from the curb one by one, moving down the road in single file.

~*~

Tommy heard an angry buzzing sound in the distance, growing louder. A half-dozen sport motorcycles flew up behind the youths and screeched to a halt. The leather-clad riders put their booted feet down to steady their bikes in unison.

Moses climbed from the back of the lead bike, pulled off his helmet, and addressed the teens. "You kids get the fuck out of here. Now."

The kids continued to eye him insolently, until Lukas climbed from his bike, presenting a much more menacing figure.

Tommy holstered his gun. The boys waved at him and moved grudgingly along. When they were a safe distance away, Moses went around the corner and entered the cemetery.

"Can't you ever stay the fuck out of trouble?" he asked Tommy as he approached.

"I didn't start it! What's with the escort?"

"I saw this coming when I was walking down the street. Ran back home and had Lukas round up his crew. As you can see, they're well-known around here. Saved your ass, Tommy."

"Fuck that. I had the situation under control."

"Bullshit, you were like General Custer at Little Big Horn. Outnumbered and out-gunned." They both laughed at the analogy. "You still want to talk?"

"Tell you what; I might've shit myself a little. I'm going to head home, and I'll come over to your place later if that's okay. I'm having second thoughts about us meeting in public. I thought if there was a safe place, it would be the cemetery. So much for that idea. Should have stuck with Wyla's."

"See ya later," Moses said. He signaled to the bikers to wait and headed back in their direction.

Tommy looked at the etched portrait of Jesus on the headstone, with its halo, loving expression, and outstretched hands. "And what do you think, Son of God? What should I do with your priest, your man of God? Why haven't you dealt with him? Why has he been allowed to harm those kids?"

There was silence. No responses came into his head, as they had in the conversation with his dead partner. "You know what I think? Maybe, just maybe, that's what my purpose is. Maybe it's you who's compelling me to take this action. Maybe I am your vigilante angel in this cesspool of humanity."

Tommy pulled out his folding knife and dug the rock from the earth. It was much larger than the protruding tip had led him to believe. He refilled and smoothed the earth over the spot, bringing it back into harmony with its surroundings.

Then he stood, placed the rock on the headstone, and made his way to the car.

I have my answer.

1 HIGH ON DRUGS

TOMMY DROVE SLOWLY through the blighted neighborhood he once patrolled. *The streets never change.* Tough kids hanging out on the crumbling stoops eyed him boldly. He realized he was in his old-white-guy Buick, not his black-and-white police cruiser.

He wondered how many generations of cops had patrolled here, and how many generations manned those same stoops in defiance. *Like a wheel that keeps turning, we live and die, come and go in shifts. It never ends.*

He was starting to understand now, finally, why they were all so angry. He scanned the building numbers, counting to himself to compensate for the gaps since most of them were no longer marked. When he knew he was close, he pulled against the curb and got out of the car, locking it up. It was late afternoon, and he wanted to be out of the neighborhood by dark. *That's when the monsters come out.*

A row of sport bikes in various states of decay were backed up to the curb. He walked to the bottom of the steps and looked up at the young men standing and sitting around the vestibule entrance above him. They wore jeans, work boots, and black leather vests emblazoned with 'Black Eagles' chest patches. He recognized them as his saviors from earlier in the day. *You remember the drill: act like you belong. Don't show weakness or fear.*

"Thanks for the assist this afternoon, fellas." They looked at him silently. "Nice bikes. I used to ride; had a sweet Harley. No Harleys, fellas?"

"That's some broke-down racist bikes. Not for the brothers. Too damn slow," one of them replied.

"Moses lives here?" Tommy asked.

The oldest-looking and largest of the three pushed his cigarette out on the crumbling brick wall and came forward. "We don't talk to the law around here. Gets us locked up, even if we done nothing wrong."

Tommy leaned forward and put his foot on the first step. "Used to be the law, remember? Could still be though, if it comes down to it. I hear they're hiring, you guys should apply. Everyone should spend a year in the military or as a cop. Teaches discipline."

The leader scoffed. "Everyone should spend a year being black. Teaches *reality*." His friends laughed.

"Yeah. Anyway, I'm a friend, he's expecting me."

The big youth stood his ground, flanked by two others, and they blocked the entrance. "You don't look like no friend of Uncle Mos. You look like a man come to serve a warrant or some shit. Friends don't look like you around here. Uncle Mos said nothin' about visitors, especially old cracker visitors."

Tommy became frustrated. "Jesus, fellas. We met already, at Wyla's, remember? I was with him…"

There was a scraping sound; they all looked up at the slowly rising window sash above them.

Two large black hands planted themselves on the gray concrete sill. The rest of Moses Taylor's head emerged, topped by the gray remains of a once-proud afro, now devastated by chemotherapy. He looked around like an ancient turtle patiently investigating its surroundings. They all waited until he spoke.

"Lukas, dammit, are you boys fucking with my guest?"

"No, Uncle Mos. Just making sure everything is alright," the leader called up to him.

Moses looked down at the group. "Don't play with that white man. Something wrong with that motherfucker. Ain't right in the head. Let him pass." He retracted his head and pulled the sash back down.

Tommy continued up the steps. As the young men parted, the leader spoke to him again. "Your car's awful close to that hydrant, mister. How 'bout you leave me your keys? We do valet service 'round here."

Tommy laughed. "Not a chance. Tell you what though, you fellas make sure nothing happens to my ride, and I'll take care of you on the way out." He pulled his keys from his jacket pocket, dangled them for a moment, and then replaced them and continued into the building. *Street logic. Still got it, old boy.*

At the top of the rickety stairs, a door creaked open, and Tommy moved toward it. Moses stood—or rather stooped—in the doorway. The men met in a light embrace. *He's getting frailer by the day.* Tommy felt Moses' ribs through his thin shirt as they briefly hugged each other.

Moses shuffled over to a well-worn easy chair and sagged into it. He motioned for Tommy to sit on the couch.

Tommy closed the door and took in the room. The place was a collage of the memories and possessions of a man who used to be but was no more. Faded posters of music idols—Marley, Gil-Scott Heron, and Hendrix—curled away from the walls just like the paint. The television was from another era but tuned to today's news, the volume low. The room, like its occupant, had a sadness to it; as if it had lived and already died.

"Don't mind those young guns out there," Moses said. "They're good. My nephew Lukas and a few of the others work over at the VA hospital." A small white dog bounded into the room and jumped onto his lap.

"Nice dog," Tommy said.

"Yeah, Whitey is a comfort dog, I guess. A man can't get a more loving friend. No matter what you are, any kind of piece of shit, broke, sick, whatever, a dog's gonna love you. I wish people could be like that." He pointed to a bottle wrapped in a brown paper bag on the coffee table. "Have a hit?"

Tommy reached over and slid it out of its sheath far enough to read the label, then pulled it all the way out and sat it on the table. The purple liquid inside and cluster of grapes on the label were familiar to him from his days on the street.

"Mad Dog 20/20 in a skirt. What the hell are you drinking that rot-gut for, Moses? That shit is bum wine."

Moses laughed and examined it lovingly. "It's cheap, gets my drunk on light and easy, and it ain't like I have to worry about my health no more." He picked it up, unscrewed the cap, and pulled long and hard. He replaced the cap and cradled it.

"I like the grape, Tommy. Taste of this reminds me of the sacramental wine at the church. I used to hit on that when nobody was looking when I was helping my dad clean up after services. I'd put a little water back in so nobody knew but me and the good Lord."

Tommy gestured toward a book on the table—*The Odyssey*. "Wow, that's some deep shit. You actually reading it or is it just to impress lady visitors?"

"Already done read it all. Twice. I love that stuff. When you get into it, you get a sense history keeps repeating itself. And we don't learn a damn thing."

Tommy changed the subject. "How you doing, Mos? You up to this? I'm thinking maybe we should let it go. Maybe we're too old for this vigilante shit."

Moses looked at him with jaundiced eyes. "I'm sick, and I'm tired, Chief, but I got enough left in me for this. Motherfucker needs to pay. I want to leave this world knowing I did something right. He won't hurt nobody after we're done, and I'll see that son of a bitch in hell. Shouldn't nobody be hurting kids like that."

He slid open a drawer in the coffee table, extracted a tin box, and pulled the lid off with a metallic pop. Tommy eyed the contents. Cellophane bags were neatly rolled and stacked in the bed of the box like the cannelloni his grandmother used to make. He suddenly realized he was starving.

Moses selected a bag and pulled an album sleeve from a rack next to his chair. "Santana, *Abraxas*. Man, I love me some Santana." He placed it on his lap and dumped the weed from the bag onto it, sifting the seeds out with a playing card. Tommy looked on, fascinated by the man's deft movements as he pulled rolling papers from the tin and fashioned a perfect joint.

Moses looked up. "You gonna bust me, copper?"

"Nah, shit. Maybe back in the day. That stuff's almost legal now anyway."

"Good, because this here is medicinal grade. Works wonders for the nausea. Course, I been smoking it since long before I got sick," Moses said with a laugh. He pulled a small vial that looked like nail polish from the tin, removed the top and painted a long black stripe down the length of the joint. "Hash oil; a little something extra for the head."

He placed the joint in the lid to dry, pulled the black vinyl album from the sleeve and started it up on his ancient stereo. Returning to his chair, he lit the joint, took a drag and looked to the ceiling before letting the smoke out in a long, thick trail. "Some for you, Chief?"

"I never…"

"You're not on the job anymore. No reason not to. If the Big C comes back and you feel as sick as I do, you'll want it. It does wonders for that constant I-gotta-puke feeling. C'mon, it's medicine." Moses pushed the joint toward Tommy.

Tommy took it, and said, "What the hell, I always wondered…" He took a former smoker's drag and held it in for a moment before coughing it out. "Jesus. That shit burns, you need a filter on the damn thing."

Moses laughed again. "Filter would take out all the good stuff, my man." They sat without talking, passing it back and forth.

Tommy became incredibly relaxed. The last of the setting sun streamed in through the window and seemed to give the drab room new life, bathing it in a reverent orange glow. The men on the posters seemed to come to life and join him in the room.

"Damn, this sure is a nice buzz. Nice and mellow. Tell me again, Mos, why is a violence-inducing drug like alcohol legal and this shit isn't?"

"You asking me, copper?"

"Damn," Tommy said. "I can't think right."

"Then there ain't no change so far?"

Tommy laughed. His mind opened in a way he'd never experienced before—to the beauty of the world, and the mystery of their existence on it. He picked up the colorful album cover and studied it. "What's this all about? What's with the naked black chick and naked red angel chick with the conga drum between her legs?"

"It's a painting, inspired by the biblical story of the Annunciation. That's when the angel Gabriel appeared to the Virgin Mary and told her that in nine months she would have a baby, the Son of God."

"So...the black woman is the Virgin Mary? I'm not saying nothin', I learned my lesson with you that first day in the hospital." They both laughed at the memory, and Tommy replaced the album cover.

"Mos—you ever think about aliens?"

"Huh? You mean like illegal aliens or little green men aliens?"

"Little green men. Do you think they're out there? I mean—why not, right?"

"Damn sure if they are, they're probably looking down at us in amazement. A whole planet of motherfuckers slaughtering each other for thousands of years over whose crazy-ass ancient stories are real when in reality none of them are."

"Sometimes I wonder if maybe we aren't the defects from some alien race, exiled to this planet a long time ago. We're so different from any other form of life here."

The descending darkness outside was interrupted when a light switched on in the apartment opposite, its window facing Tommy and just a few yards away. Tommy watched as a slim, attractive woman began to undress.

"Damn, Mos. You didn't tell me there was a show."

"She's always doing that. Just lonely, I guess, or wanting attention. I see her walking with her man, and that's one dude I wouldn't want to catch me peeping on his wife, even if she's begging. I don't pay her much mind. She's not my Angie."

"That's how I want to be," Tommy replied. "I want to be virtuous like you, Mos."

Tommy pried his eyes away from the scene and sat back, melting into the old, comfortable couch with his eyes closed. The words and music from the stereo seemed to become part of his consciousness. The songs were familiar, but he heard instruments and background vocals he never knew were there before. He'd heard the song "What's Goin' On" by Marvin Gaye before but never stopped to listen to what it was about. It saddened him to think about the brutality it spoke of, and that he'd been guilty of it back then. *Different times.*

He awoke sometime later, looked over to find Moses sleeping, and got up and let himself out quietly.

Lukas and the other youths were leaning against his car. He pulled the keys from his pocket and clicked the fob button to unlock the doors. He approached Lukas.

The youth stood back and made a grandiose gesture toward the car. "Good as gold, Pops."

Tommy remembered his promise and pulled a twenty from his wallet. He handed it to the man. "Don't spend it on any bullshit that's going to fuck your life up. Your uncle's a good man; do him proud."

The young man stepped away from the car, and Tommy put his hand out. The youth made a fist instead and extended it until Tommy caught on and bumped his own fist against it. "Germs, bro," Lukas said as he walked away, stuffing the twenty in his pocket.

On the ride home, Tommy turned on the Buick's radio for the first time in forever. He found stations he didn't know existed and turned the volume up. He found the bass control, increased it, and enjoyed the thumping vibration. The traffic lights seemed brighter than he ever remembered, and he was very hungry.

~*~

When he pulled into the driveway, he cut the engine but stayed in the car long enough for "Stairway to Heaven" to come to its end, singing the final verse with flagrant hand gestures. He looked up and saw Bobby in the window, watching him and shaking his head.

He entered the house and climbed the stairs to Bobby's room. His son seemed startled when he entered; Tommy rarely visited him in his own space.

"What's up, Dad? The last time you were in here, I think it was to read me a bedtime story."

"Easy, son. Can't the old man stop by without the third degree? What's that you're working on?" Tommy inspected the elaborate, half-finished fantasy drawing on his son's desk. It was a vibrant mountainous landscape dotted with castles, and with dragons flying through the air. "It's amazing; the detail is so intricate," he said. "You should do something with this talent, son."

"Wow," Bobby said. "That's the first time you've encouraged me to be anything but a cop. You feeling okay, Dad?"

"Never been better, son, never been better. Where's your mother?"

"She's at Aunt Diane's. She said she'll be home in about an hour."

Tommy went downstairs and dug around in his wife's cookbooks until he found a recipe scrawled on an old sheet of notebook paper. He went to the living room and opened the lid to their wooden casket-sized stereo entertainment center. He pulled an old 8-track tape from the internal rack and slid it into the player slot with a plastic click, then twisted the volume knob. The first strains of Bruce Springsteen's "Born to Run" boomed out as he entered the kitchen pantry.

He selected ingredients while shuffling to the music and belting out lyrics.

"Sprung from cages out on highway nine...stewed tomatoes!

"It's a death trap! It's a suicide rap!...extra virgin olive oil!

"We'll run till we drop, baby we'll never go back!...pasta shells!"

A shadow fell over him, and he spun around. Margie stood in the doorway, her hands on her hips. Bobby was behind her, looking over her shoulder.

"What are you doing? What the hell is wrong with you?" she shouted over the music. Bobby walked over to the casket and turned the volume down. Other than the muted music, silence prevailed while she waited for his response.

He stood there defenseless, the recipe in one hand and a box of pasta in the other, his euphoria exposed. "I'm making Grandma's cannelloni. I'm damn hungry, for a change, and I'm craving it." He felt foolish and ashamed to know they'd been watching him. His joy evaporated as if someone had sucked it up with a vacuum. He was cornered in the pantry, Margie blocking the door.

She peered at him suspiciously. "What the hell have you been up to? What's wrong with your eyes? Bobby said you smelled like dope when you came in, and you were acting all funny. What are you, stupid?"

His embarrassment turned to rage, and his mellow buzz was gone. "Stupid, huh? You think I'm stupid? I'm enjoying myself for the first time since I got sick, and you have to step on me? I'm gonna die. Being happy for once is *acting funny*?"

He stopped to glare at her, and she remained silent. "You don't think I know where you been? Over to your sister's, drinking with her again? You never stopped, I know. I know about your stash up there in the cupboard. I didn't do nothing wrong. I went to visit Paulie's grave. He was a saint, that man. Then I visited Moses—he's not doing well. That's all. And you're still a goddamn drunk, Margie."

He had revealed what they had both tacitly agreed to ignore for so long. He could smell the booze on her.

She countered with her own angry response. "That man was no saint. You think he was a saint? There's a lot you don't know. Nobody's a saint in this world, but he was a good man, and I miss him too. I miss him a lot."

She paused, as if considering her next words, and she began to cry. "More than you know, Tommy. We dreamed of someday being together without having to hide. He died because of you, and now you're going to die too." She whirled, sobbing, grabbed her purse from the kitchen table and went out the door.

Bobby stood back in the living room, watching silently, as he always did when they fought. He called out to his father. "Dad…"

Tommy didn't turn to face him. "Go. Leave me alone."

Bobby walked toward the stairway back up to his bedroom.

Tommy stood there in the pantry, letting the revelation wash over him, feeling he had nowhere to go and nobody to turn to. He replaced the ingredients and walked out as Springsteen's last whispers finished the song.

Come on with me, tramps like us, baby we were born to run.

He pulled the 8-track from the slot, and it jammed, trailing a stream of tape like brown spaghetti. *Son of a bitch, I liked that one.* He threw it into the console and closed the lid.

He lay down on the formal couch, unused except for the rare company they had, and closed his eyes. The clear vinyl protective cover squeaked as he tried to get comfortable.

Moments later he rose, plucked his jacket from the peg next to the door and left.

~*~

Tommy scanned the sea of empty tables in the hospital cafeteria and chose one. He sat with his coffee and took note of the exhausted graveyard-shift workers on their breaks—doctors, nurses, maintenance people, cafeteria workers, aides. The full spectrum of income levels and employment for a building full of sick, desperate people. *Real heroes.*

He wished he could go upstairs and find his friends all there, and have their comfort and camaraderie to soothe his wounded soul. But it was late; he'd come down long ago from the effects of the drug, and he was exhausted.

"You lost, young man?"

He turned to see who it was, but he already recognized the accent and the soft, caring tone. "Nurse Carmen, what the hell are you doing here this late?"

The angel in white took a seat opposite him. "I'm pulling some extra shifts. We've got to get that piece-of-shit car squared away."

Tommy thought about the contrast of her pristine appearance with that of her boyfriend and car. "What's the deal with you and that guy? I still don't see any ring."

Carmen looked down and touched her ring finger as if expecting it to be there. "I did have one, like I said. We're engaged. It was my mother's, simple and nice. Buster had to hock it. We needed the money."

The words touched Tommy and made him angry at the same time. "Carmen, Jesus. You can do better, kid. What kind of man doesn't work to support his family? What the hell does he do all day?"

Carmen seemed caught between anger at the truth and her natural inclination to support her man. "Yeah, it's always been excuses and promises with him. I've always believed it, or wanted to, anyway. My patience was wearing thin, but for some reason, he's being nicer lately."

"Really?"

"Yeah, it's tough on him. My father has to live with us, and it's difficult. He's got Alzheimer's. Not long ago he grabbed me up and shook me. He wouldn't let go, and Buster had to pull him off."

"Oh, damn…" Tommy said. *Whoops.* He switched gears to fatherly advice. "Move on, Carmen. You're beautiful, caring, and have a good career ahead of you. You're a natural nurse. And a good mom, I'm sure."

"I don't have any kids, Tommy. Not yet, anyway."

He realized that Vela had been lying back in the warehouse, as he'd suspected at the time. *He's still a piece of shit, either way. He doesn't deserve her. She deserves better.*

She smiled a weary smile at him. "My momma died from cancer. I was there every step of the way. I was just a little girl, so I had to grow up fast. I learned to care for her at home, giving her injections into her belly, feeding her. She wasted away until all I could recognize of her was her voice through the moaning.

"She made it through that Christmas, gave me a Barbie camper. I wanted that damn thing so bad but never wanted to ask. We didn't have the money. I still don't know how she found out I wanted it. Probably intercepted my letter to Santa. I still have it—beat up as hell, not much better than my real car."

She looked down again. "She died at home, with only me and my brothers and sisters there. When it happened, we were like lost puppies circling her, sad and confused. Anyway, that's why I wanted to be a nurse. Actually, a doctor.

"I don't want to talk about me so much. What about you? What the hell *are* you doing here this late? Can't get enough of this place?"

Tommy shifted in the uncomfortable, rickety cafeteria chair. It squeaked, and he started, worried she might've thought it was him. She looked at him quizzically until she figured it out.

"Chair," he said, repeating the action to confirm, and they both laughed. It momentarily broke the tension. "Domestic trouble, I guess you could say. Shit really hit the fan tonight. Some new wounds inflicted, and old wounds reopened. She's a drunk, I knew that much. What I didn't know was that she was doing my late partner on the beat."

Carmen put her hand on his shoulder and looked him in the eye. "Listen, Tommy. We're all flawed. I'm betting you did some things she never found out about. Cops are notorious for that stuff, right? Didn't you hit on me, mister?"

"I did, but it was vanity. I'd never do anything; I'm too principled. The flesh is always tempted, but my virtue is strong. That's the Corps in me. Not that I had a shot with someone like you. I was trying to get my ego stroked, a desperate old man is all."

"Okay. But she stuck it out with you. She's sticking this out with you now. One thing my patients always forget is that this is hard on their loved ones, too. Go on home, Tommy. Make amends. Life is too short."

He drained his coffee, then rose to leave. He embraced her, thanked her, and deposited his Styrofoam cup into the trash on the way out.

Don't I know it.

~*~

The muffled jukebox music found its way out of the squat brick building and into the mind and memories of the man in the car parked in front. Keeping his eyes closed allowed him to more effectively travel back to the time and place each song invoked. *That juke always had the best records in it.*

Percy Sledge sang "When a Man Loves a Woman," and in his mind he stood in the high school gym, senior year, trying to work up the courage to ask pretty Margie Madison to dance. The dance was almost over, and the previous three slow ones had resulted in someone else getting to her first. The Marine Corps and Vietnam lay ahead. This time he started off in a determined march across the floor to her. *She was all I ever wanted.*

The memory faded like mist as Tommy opened his eyes. He placed his hand on the car door handle. A small voice inside him begged for the courage not to go into the tavern and feed his addiction all over again.

Murphy's Tavern. So long ago, it seems. He looked at the faded green neon sign above the entrance and thought about the problems he'd tried to wash away inside. *And all the problems I caused by spending so much time in there.*

The song changed, pulling his reverie forward, years later. The place was full of cops getting loaded before going home to angry spouses, sleeping children, and cold dinners. *All of us driving home shit-faced after spending the day busting people for the same thing. Most of us turning slowly into alcoholics.*

He put himself back, in penance, to a particular drunken night. With Paulie egging him on, he came up behind the barmaid and cupped her breasts through her shirt. He remembered turning to find Margie standing in the doorway, horrified and crying. *I never would've done anything, honey. I loved you.*

He brought himself back to the present and remembered what Margie had revealed hours earlier about his best friend. *You dirty son of a bitch, Paulie...*

He kept his eyes closed. The explosive beginning strains of "Light My Fire" by the Doors filtered out. They put him back at the Marine Khe Sanh combat base and the nightmare of the Tet Offensive. Rapid-fire images came flooding back to him. Friends blown to pieces. Picking up those pieces and stuffing them into body bags. Trying not to die.

Calling out to Margie, who was halfway around the world, nobody able to hear him crying in the deafening roar of combat in the jungle.

He opened his eyes again. He could see the shadows of movement through the glass-block window of the bar. The urge for a drink, to be on a comfortable leather barstool watching sports with other hapless lost souls, was growing on him. He pushed it down, pushed it away, closed his eyes again to try to make it stop. *Maybe for a little bit. It's almost closing time.*

A sharp noise jolted him awake. He tried to jump up, but the still-fastened seat belt restrained him. A figure outside tapped on his driver's side window again with a stick. He rolled the window down and tried to adjust his eyes to the early dawn light. The officer asked for his license and registration. Tommy handed them over, making sure his police ID was visible in the process.

The officer leaned in closer. "Borata? What, are you on a stakeout, old timer?"

His sarcasm annoyed Tommy. "Nah, got a call from an old buddy to give him a ride home, passed out waiting for him. Guess he made other plans. I better head out and go check on him at his place."

The officer handed back the documents. "Sure thing, buddy. Stay out of trouble, okay?"

Tommy started the car and pulled down the street, unsure where he would go next.

16 DECLINE

TOMMY LEANED BACK and squinted to find his target through the glare of the rising sun. He selected another round from his cache of ammunition and fired. The pebble rose in an arc and bounced off the window pane. *Dink.* He repeated the action. *Dink. Dink.*

Finally, as he began to give in to the exhaustion of the previous night, he saw a figure moving beyond the window. The sash rose angrily, and Moses' head emerged.

"What the hell is wrong with you, cracker? You got any idea what time it is? Get the hell up here so I can whup your punk ass."

Tommy laughed as he moved toward the building entrance. He found the top of the stairs and entered the dim apartment. "Got any coffee,

brother man? Cream and sugar?" he asked
Moses, who was already at work brewing a pot.

Moses shuffled from one area of the small
kitchen to another. His spoon created a pleasant,
rhythmic tinkling against the ceramic mugs as he
stirred. "So what's the deal? You come back for
more of that good stuff you had last night?"

"Rough night, Mos. I had a good time here.
Then I went back to my place, and the shit hit the
fan with my old lady. She came back from her
sister's place loaded and started on me for having
too much fun. It got ugly. Turns out she was
banging my partner all that time, back in the day.
The one I was telling you about, that got killed on
the job.

"I stomped out, went to the hospital for a
while and hung out in the cafeteria. Carmen was
there, working an extra shift. Then I went to the
bar, but I didn't go in. Now here I am, no sleep,
exhausted."

Moses put the steaming cups on the scratched
table and sat. "I'd offer you something stronger
to drink, but I know better by now."

"Don't think I'm not tempted," Tommy said.

Moses turned the television on. He adjusted the over-air antenna to pull in a better picture as the morning news program began. "Sorry," he said, as he rose with a great effort and went into the bathroom a few steps away.

The sounds of his vomiting mixed with the drone of the news update.

"You need help in there, Mos?" There was no reply, only the sound of misery from behind the door.

There was a stumble and crash, followed by what sounded like an explosion of gastrointestinal gases. Tommy rose and yanked the bathroom door open, and was immediately overcome by the stench of feces and vomit. It brought him back to the war-zone hospital tents in Vietnam. *Shit and puke splattered everywhere.* His friend sat naked on the commode, slumping to one side, moaning.

"Get out, get out, give me some damn dignity, you asshole," Moses said.

"Fuck that. You need help. Give me a minute." Tommy exited, ran across the room and retched out of the open window. He opened the other windows, then removed his t-shirt, wrapped it around his face, and tied it behind his head. He went back into the bathroom, turning on the fan and then the tub faucet full blast.

Moses looked at him. "What the fuck is this, cracker? Home invasion? Get the fuck out and let me deal with my own business."

Tommy grabbed him under the arm. "Get up. Get in the tub. I'll take care of this. That's a fucking order. Do it, now."

Moses complied while Tommy gathered cleaning supplies. He worked fast, occasionally ducking out to gulp down fresh air. During one trip, as he stuck his head out of the window, he saw Lukas outside working on his motorcycle, looking up at him.

"What the fuck you crazy old bastards doing up there?" he asked.

Tommy didn't reply. He continued to clean, then went down the hall to the trash chute with plastic bags full of soiled paper towels and linens. As he re-entered the apartment, Moses emerged from the bathroom with a towel wrapped around him.

"I had to throw some of that shit out, Mos. I'll replace it. You okay?"

"Not really, brother. Mr. C is coming to get me now, I feel it. I took all my damn pills this morning, then I puked them all up without them doing no good. It's a losing proposition."

Moses went to his bedroom to change. Tommy lit some incense sticks and placed them into a teak holder.

Moses returned and sagged into his recliner. "What's the deal with our friend the priest?"

"This motherfucker is going to walk away, that's what. That's the Church, no doubt. They pay someone off, so they don't get sued, then reassign his ass somewhere else just like they said they would. Like they always do. He'll go right back to hurting other kids."

Moses opened his tin box, removed a joint, positioned it between his lips, and flipped his lighter on with a pop. He leaned back into the frayed chair and drew deep. As the stream of smoke exited through his nose, he said, "Now that's the shit." He passed the joint to Tommy.

Tommy took a light hit. "We got to do something, Mos, if he's still in that rectory."

"I don't know, Tommy. I'm getting sicker. Time is short for me, and you're getting better.

You may have this beat. Why risk going to prison? It could be a long stretch."

They passed the joint between them as they spoke. Tommy lingered on the question, and then responded, "Nobody beats this. It's a matter of time. We talked about this remission bullshit. It's a temporary oasis, a short summer before a long, final winter.

"Listen, Mos. Something I didn't tell you. I think I'm figuring it out now. Maybe I didn't want to think about it all these years. That priest, he was in our parish way back. My kid, Bobby, was an altar boy right around that time..."

He stopped, as pieces of possibilities swirled and formed themselves together in his addled mind. He wished he hadn't smoked; he was getting emotional at the theory that was presenting itself. He began to cry as he forced more words out.

"My boy, Bobby. He's a good kid. Not quite like me in a lot of ways, but he's my boy, you know?"

Moses carefully stabbed the remains of the joint into an ashtray and saved it in the tin box. "He's a good kid, you got that right. Cherish that.

I never got to have any kids. That's why I took to mentoring that crew outside. Those are my kids, and they're alright."

"Right," Tommy continued. "But the thing is, he's never had any girlfriends, no interest. That's kind of strange, right? Gets pissed if I push him on it. Maybe I've been in denial about the obvious. These are different times, right? But, you see, I'm wondering now, he was around that priest, maybe…"

Moses interrupted. "Hold on now. Whether anything happened with that priest or not, he didn't make your kid gay. You're jumping to a lot of conclusions there, Chief. Go easy. You got to talk to your boy."

Tommy scowled. It was too much for him. He wiped the moisture away from his eyes with a sleeve. "Well if that happened, the priest has got to pay. Either way, there's a lot of parents right now, and kids, whose lives were ruined because of that son of a bitch. I'm going to put it together, Mos. If you aren't ready for this, I can pull it off. He's got to pay. I ain't got much to live for, and it would feel damn good."

"Talk to your boy first. That's what's important now. If something happened, it could break the case open if he'll talk about it. If he's traumatized, he might need help. Those are the priorities. On the other side, if you come up with something, come back to me with it. But this old black man is running out of gas soon. I got an appointment this afternoon with the doc."

Tommy lay down on the couch. "I hear you, Mos. I'll talk to my boy. I can't go home yet, though. Things are all fucked up with this revelation about Margie and my old buddy. I can't get past it. I'm so down over all this, Mos. I'm so tired. You mind if I stretch out here and crash for a while?"

"No worries at all, my brother from another mother. Make yourself comfortable. Go use the bedroom if you want."

Within minutes, Tommy was snoring. Moses covered him with a blanket and pulled up a chair to the window to look out over his world.

17 AN OPTION

MOSES AND TOMMY SAT in the oncology waiting room. Other patients, and their younger friends and family members, sat passing the time while waiting for their names to be called. The young were consumed by electronics; the old read books and magazines. Some sat staring into space. It was a sea of bandannas, ball caps, and flower hats perched upon chemo-ravaged heads. Some wore paper masks over their noses and mouths.

An aura of sadness permeated the room. Most looked like they were already dead, or wished they were. The faded, beaten condition of the patients contrasted with their bright, healthy loved ones. Their hushed silence yielded to sounds from the other rooms: muffled discussions, the beeping of medical equipment, soft crying.

The young shepherding out the old. And sometimes the reverse, Tommy thought.

Moses leaned over and whispered, "To hell with this cancer. I'm about to die from depression in here."

"How you feeling, brother? That was horrible, seeing you go through that this morning. You can't be living alone; you need help. Listen, how about I move in for a while and help you out? I'm on the outs with the old lady anyway."

Moses stared at him for a moment before responding. "I'm fine. Doc'll fix me up with some shit to take care of that. Your ass belongs home with your old lady, Tommy. Make that right. She's been by your side a long time. I wish I had my old lady back every day, my friend. And I don't need your ass snoring on my damn couch at night."

Tommy laughed. "Bullshit. You're afraid I'll catch your black ass jerking off to Diana Ross pictures." His voice had risen, and now many of the faces in the waiting room turned to them. Some smiled, but most frowned.

"As soon as I'm done in here, I got to take my friend down to the mental ward for his own appointment," Moses said to the group. They all turned back and went about their own dreary business.

A nurse walked in. "Taylor," she announced. "Moses Taylor."

Moses and Tommy rose at once. "Where the hell you going?" Moses asked.

"I'm moral support. I'm not staying out here; the place is full of sick people."

"You're a mean mofo, Mr. Borata. Come on, I guess. I can't shake you."

They followed the nurse down the hall and into a doctor's office. They sat, and she went through the routine of checking Moses' vitals and recording them on the computer.

"Why do you have to wear that mask? You can't catch what we have," Tommy asked her.

"I understand that, sir. I'm a medical professional. I have to wear the mask to prevent Mr. Taylor from getting sicker. He has a compromised immune system, and we all carry germs. I work around a lot of sick people if you didn't notice."

"Oh, okay," Tommy said, embarrassed.

"Doc will be in soon," she said as she left the room abruptly.

"Hell of a bedside manner," Tommy remarked.

Moses grunted. "You got to stop pissing people off, especially when I'm the one they're working on."

Tommy sighed. "Yeah, I get it, but it's frustrating. They sit your ass in the waiting room for an hour, then they bring you in here and damn if you don't wait in here for another hour. And not a thing to do in here, except look at your ugly ass."

"I'm the pretty one; you're the ugly bastard. Old as dirt, too."

After a while, they heard the shuffling of papers outside the door and a quick exchange of notes between the doctor and nurse.

The doctor entered and looked between Tommy and Moses. Moses introduced them.

"How are you doing, Mr. Taylor?" she asked.

"I'm fine, I guess, for a dying guy."

"Bullshit," Tommy interjected. "He's sick as hell. Vomiting and explosive diarrhea this morning."

Moses glared at him.

The doctor didn't comment. She flipped through images on her computer screen. The two men waited silently, watching her. Finally, she turned to face them.

"Mr. Taylor, as you can probably guess, this isn't good news. Would you like your friend to wait outside?"

"He stays. Let's have it."

"Your cancer is spreading. At this point, we're out of options, other than to continue with even more aggressive chemotherapy..."

Moses cut her off. "Not an option. No more chemo."

"Okay then. You will begin to decline rather quickly. I would suggest either home care or hospice. You'll soon get to the point where caring for yourself is not possible."

"I'm going to do it," Tommy burst in. He wiped his eyes with the palm of his hand. "I'll take care of him. I did it today."

"He's going to need professional care, Mr. Borata. I understand you're a vet, Moses. Many of my patients who are veterans go to the VA hospital. They get the respect they deserve and are well cared-for there. And thank you for your service."

"How long?" Moses asked. "How long before it's so bad I can't keep up?"

The doctor maintained her professional demeanor. "Probably weeks, at best. Perhaps sooner."

The men rose and left the room. On the way down the hall, Moses stopped in front of the men's room. "I got to go. It might be a while, Tommy, and I got to make a few calls from the lobby. Meet me at Wyla's. Go ahead and warm me up a seat, and I'll see you there."

Tommy embraced his friend. "Okay, my brother. You sure?"

"Unless you want to come in and wipe my ass, cracker. Shove off and let me take care of my business. Set me up with a shot and a beer."

Tommy wandered the halls in thought, trying to find his way back to the hospital exit. He found himself shuffling slowly, his problems both above and below the surface of his psyche gnawing away at his mind and spirit. *So many problems; so much sadness in this world...*

He passed by a doorway and heard a murmuring adult voice, and then that of a child. He stopped and looked at the sign above the door. *Chapel.* The door was open just a crack, and he discreetly peered in.

~*~

Moses walked through the hospital lobby. His legs could only manage a slow pace, but his mind raced with every step, trying to process his mortality.

He entered the men's room and thought about his options as he stood at the urinal. He finished and stood in front of the sink and mirror, taking stock of himself. He still had his intimidating height, but now he looked downright scary. The lost weight caused his previously form-fit clothing to hang from him. His face was gaunt, his eyes jaundiced, his crown a patchy silver-gray minefield of stubble.

The door opened, and a thin, well-dressed man entered with a small boy. The man looked at

Moses and then guided the boy back out of the door. "Let's wait," he said.

"But, Dad, I gotta *go,*" the boy said as the door swung closed behind them.

"Fuck you, buddy," Moses said aloud, although they were gone.

It sucks to be a monster.

As he re-entered the lobby, the multi-colored stuffed animals and bright flowers in the window of the hospital gift shop caught his eye. He opened the door and wandered in.

He browsed through the aisles, considering items to bring back to brighten his apartment. The fragrance of the flowers and light music coming from unseen speakers helped his mood a little. As he picked up items and inspected them, checking the price tags on the base of each, he began to feel like he was being watched.

He gazed over the top of the aisle's shelving and noticed the cashier peering at him suspiciously. Her overly pink, excessively made-up face twisted into a dour expression of disapproval, the wasted lipstick on her mouth painting an inverted smile. He ignored her and continued his search, moving into the furthest aisle away from her.

He looked through a selection of thick, soft socks, thinking about the threadbare ones he'd been wearing since his beloved Angie had passed. He glanced again toward the register and noticed that the woman wasn't there. Turning to walk further down the aisle, he almost tripped on her, as she crouched at a lower shelf, pretending to inventory its items, with her eyes still fixed on him.

"Excuse me," Moses said, as he made his way around her to the greeting card aisle.

He reviewed several friendship cards, hoping to find something to thank Tommy for helping him through his ordeal. He read a few, chuckling at the light-hearted limericks and verses.

"Sir, can I help you?"

He turned, and she was there at the head of the aisle, hands on hips.

"No, I'm just browsing," he responded bluntly. *Don't be intimidated. Don't be shooed away.*

One card in particular caught his fancy, and he placed it atop the shelf. He read several more.

"Are you going to buy something, sir?" she asked.

He'd forgotten about her, lost in the mirth presented by the simple cards. "Yes, I'm going to buy this goddamn card and get the hell out of this store," he angrily responded.

He moved to the register and waited while the woman rang up his purchase with methodical, mechanical efficiency. The smell of her dank perfume was making him nauseous, overwhelming even the nearby floral displays. *It's as ugly as her soul.*

He dug through his pants, pulling out some bills and change, and paid her, grabbing the card from the counter and heading for the door.

"You forgot your receipt," she called after him.

"Stuff it, lady."

He placed the card in his jacket pocket and sat on a couch in the lobby waiting area. He leaned back and closed his eyes, alternately considering his options and replaying the good and bad scenes and events of his life. *Too much hate in the world. Too many hateful people. Too much evil. I'm not going down slow.* He thought about all of the times he had experienced the same thing, throughout his life, and had witnessed his loved ones endure it.

He snapped awake as he was rudely shaken by the shoulder. He'd fallen asleep, and for a moment was unsure where he was.

"You've got to move along. We don't allow loitering here. Find another place to hang out, buddy."

He turned to find a hospital security guard standing behind him. He saw the cashier staring out of the gift shop window behind the guard. When he caught her gaze, she quickly ducked away from the window. He turned his attention to the guard.

"What, you think I'm some homeless guy hanging out here to keep warm?" he asked.

The short, elderly, white-haired guard tried to give him a hardened look. "C'mon buddy. We deal with it all the time. You folks figure this is a warm, safe joint, but we can't have you taking up all the furniture."

Moses looked around the lobby. He pointed to a woman dozing on a nearby chair. "What about her? She's homeless too, right?"

"Of course not."

"Why, because she's not black?" Moses demanded.

"Look, do you have business here or not, pal?"

"I damn sure do. My business is that I'm *dying*, I just got out of my appointment in oncology. And you better watch how you talk to people, *buddy*, or you're gonna be in the dying business yourself."

With that, he rose and leered down at the guard, who now appeared to be intimidated. The guard reached for his shoulder intercom.

"Save it," Moses said, as he headed for the exit.

It's always been the same. All these years since I was a little boy. My parents, their parents, ain't a damn thing changed in all these years.

~*~

The priest placed his hand on the child's shoulder and rubbed it. It was always his first move to break the physical barrier, and it had served him well.

He evoked his most soothing tone, cupping and lifting the small boy's chin in order to force eye contact, engaging trust. "I'm sorry about your father, young man. I understand that he won't be with us much longer. I know it's difficult for someone your age to comprehend, but often this is simply God's will. Your parents asked me to talk to you in order to help you understand this."

The boy slapped the priest's hand away from his face. The priest took the opportunity to let it land on the boy's knee and continued his massage.

"My dad is good! He never hurt anyone. He went to church every week. How could God want my dad dead?" the boy demanded.

"These are things we are not permitted to ask, my son. God has a plan for all of us, both in this world and after. I believe he needs your dad in Heaven with him."

The boy had his head down again, sniffling. "Who's going to do things with me? My mom doesn't give a crap about me. She's always away for work."

The priest moved closer and placed his arm around him. "Do you like the woods, the outdoors? Camping?"

The boy kept his head down, but his voice perked up. "Yeah, my dad and I used to go camping...before he got sick."

Bingo, the priest thought. "Wonderful. I'll talk to your mom about getting you into the Scouts. They do a lot of cool things and a lot of camping. I used to be a Scoutmaster, and sometimes I still help out."

The boy looked up. "Really?"

The priest, sensing his opening, hugged the boy even tighter. "Absolutely. If they don't have a trip soon, maybe you and I can go together, just to get back into practice. And I'll let your mom know that you can hang out with me when she's away if she doesn't have anyone to watch you."

"There's just my grandma, but she's kind of old and doesn't hear good. She can't do anything."

The priest thought he saw a shadow through the opaque window in the hospital chapel door and lowered his voice just in case. "Good, good. I can't take the place of your dad, but I'll be like a big brother. We'll be best buddies, and we'll have the best time..."

He was interrupted by an angry-looking older man bursting through the door. "You!" he shouted.

Startled, the boy rose and left hurriedly through the open door.

Shit. He knows. The priest started to ask how he could help, but the man was on him in an instant, grabbing a fistful of his tunic, popping off the dog collar and yanking him to his feet.

"What are you doing here?" the man demanded. "You're supposed to be away from kids, Tarat." They were face to face, until the man reached back with his foot to close the door and then threw the priest back into the couch.

"Calm down please, sir," the priest requested. "And it's Goodman, Father Goodman." He motioned to the nameplate on his desk.

The man stood menacingly over him, confusion mingling with the rage in his expression. "What? No. You're Tarat. I know you, you son of a bitch. You fucking pervert…"

The priest's mind raced, trying to find a solution. *I always find a solution.* The man was familiar to him, and finally, he was able to reconcile the face with a name.

"Mr...Borata, correct?"

"Never mind who I am. Answer my question, motherfucker."

The priest smiled at him, confident now. "A simple name change is all. One has a right to a certain amount of privacy, especially an innocent man."

"Innocent my ass..."

"Now, now, Mr. Borata. That's no way to talk to a man of God."

"Man of God? Bullshit. You're no man of God."

"There is no God, Mr. Borata. It's just a job like yours was. You can't say you were a very good cop, now can you?"

The man was turning redder, the priest noted. *Good. Anger creates mistakes.*

"Fuck you. How do you know who I am, you sick bastard?"

"A good priest always knows his flock. It's a shame you couldn't join us more often, Mr. Borata. But I did enjoy your son's visits. Bobby, wasn't it?" he taunted.

The man appeared stunned, precisely the effect the priest had hoped for. He could almost feel the wheels turning in the man's brain, perhaps putting things together for the first time, and Father Tarat took great satisfaction from his expression. He started to smile when he was yanked off his feet again.

"Did you hurt my boy? Did you hurt my fucking kid?" the man spat in his face.

The priest remained smug, unconcerned about the threat. He whispered this time, "If I did, you would be well served to leave things in the past, like your boy has, and let bygones be bygones. For example, you wouldn't like his life to be upended by embarrassing pictures of a precocious young man getting into circulation..."

The man grabbed the priest's throat and pushed him over the desk backward, squeezing with all of the power he could summon. The priest didn't struggle; he just continued to smile.

The door popped open as a hospital administrator stuck her head in. "What the hell is going on in here?" She stared at the two as they rose from their positions.

"Do you know who this is?" the man asked.

The priest intervened. "Now, sir. Let's be careful. I suppose I could file assault charges. We do have a witness here…"

The man pushed past the administrator and left, hands clutching the sides of his head.

"Are you alright, Father Goodman?" the administrator asked.

"It's okay. Everyone has their own way of dealing with grief. He'll come to accept what he cannot change."

She left, and the priest began to gather his things. *I should've relocated. It's time to get out of Dodge.*

~*~

They sat at Wyla's long, empty bar. Lucius was busy closing blinds and turning on the exterior lighting as darkness fell. The drum-roll of the rain on the aluminum awning outside got louder as he opened the door and then shut it.

"This fucking weather is depressing," Moses said.

Tommy sat next to him, catatonic. A neglected cup of coffee slowly cooled in front of him.

"Listen, Tommy…I know this is a hard thing to digest. I can't even imagine. That night, Thanksgiving, at the shelter, I talked to your boy some about this…"

Tommy snapped out of his stupor. "You knew? You fucking knew?" he shouted.

"Hold on," Moses replied. "He implied something had happened…"

"Why didn't you tell me? Why didn't Bobby tell me?"

"I had no details, Tommy, and he didn't want to go into it. I was focused on how he was doing, not all of that. He's come to terms with it to some extent, but he's angry. I asked him to talk to you about it, to open up. He said he couldn't a long time ago, that you wouldn't have accepted it, would've blamed him…"

Tommy began to cry. "He's right, too. He's damn right. I wasn't there for him. I wondered why he changed all of a sudden. I ridiculed him, called him names…"

"He understands all of that. It's a tough thing for any family. He loves you, Tommy."

"I don't know what to do, Moses. I have to go home and talk to him and figure out what to do about this.

"A lot more than the weather is depressing. Maybe God is in nature like the Indians believed, and this weather is the second coming. Maybe it'll be a natural rapture, and the Earth will reject us all like the cancer we've been on this planet."

"I don't think I'll be around long enough for all that," Moses said.

"I'm only a lap behind you anyway. Let's figure this out together. I need you to help me get through this, Mos."

Moses didn't answer for a while; he appeared lost in thought.

"Yeah, together," Moses said. "Maybe you can take me around tomorrow to the VA hospice unit and check out what that's like, and some of those other places they talked about. We'll have a nice day of it, picking out a place for me to die."

"Of course I'll take you around. Don't jump to conclusions, though. I know it sounds bad, but you hear all these stories, right? Where people say the doc told them they had a month and they're still around five years later?"

Lucius put another shot and beer in front of Moses, stacked up the empties and took them away. "You okay?" he asked Tommy.

"Not really, Lucius, but nothing else for me right now, thanks," Tommy responded.

They sat in silence, watching sports on the television overhead.

"Anyway, forget about the priest. He'll get his. Focus on your boy," Moses said, slurring as he spoke.

They'd been quiet for so long that the comment startled Tommy. He realized it was getting late.

"Don't worry about that right now either, Mos. You're sick, you have to focus on you and nothing else. He damn sure isn't going to the same place you are."

"I don't see you letting this go. I think you got a plan, and you're cutting me out."

"You heard the doc today. I don't want you in this. You don't need the stress right now. Besides, I lied to you that night. I never killed anyone. I can't be sure, anyway. I was a bad shot in 'Nam. And like you said, that priest is probably long gone."

"So that means I'm fired, huh? You going to do this without me? Bullshit," Moses answered.

"No, no. Not like that. Let's take a break from thinking about it."

Moses leaned back and fished for something in his pocket. "I have something for you, Chief." He pulled out a gold medallion on a long chain and handed it to Tommy.

Tommy admired it. "What's this? Saint Michael? Listen, Mos—you know I don't believe…"

"Yeah, I know. You're no saint. Neither is Saint Michael. He's an archangel. He's your type of guy. He's a spiritual warrior—he was all about fighting evil and protecting the innocent. He's a vigilante, and the patron saint of cops and military."

"Wow. Sounds good to me, brother." Tommy put the chain over his neck, then unbuttoned his top shirt buttons so it would be visible. He admired himself in the clouded mirror behind the bar. "I like it."

Moses excused himself and headed to the men's room.

Lucius came over and removed his headphones. "He's not doing too well, is he?" he asked Tommy.

"No. Not good at all, Lucius." They could hear the sounds of retching from behind the flimsy men's room door.

Moses returned and downed another shot, then drained his beer. "Let's get the fuck out of here. Give me a ride home, please, and then get your ass home to your kid. I need time alone right now, Tommy. And you need to get things right with Bobby and Margie. She's probably worried sick about where you been all day."

"She'd never think to look here, that's for damn sure."

Tommy settled up the tab, including his usual generous tip.

They were halfway to Moses's place when Tommy decided to break the ice. "You know what; this life here is a temporary thing, Moses. We're completely forgotten about after what, two generations? We think the bugs have it bad, some of them only live a day or two. It's the same shit for us. Life is like a quick blink of light. What comes after for us is forever, I think. I hope. Maybe we can hang out there, in eternity."

Moses thought for a few minutes and then answered, "Listen. The way I look at it, everything in this world is now irrelevant for me. You're right. Now I see how temporary all this is, all our problems and struggles. I'm going to find out the answer to the biggest mysteries in the world. Soon I'm going to find out what comes after this. I'm going to meet God and Jesus if they exist. I'm going to find out if there's aliens."

He paused to reflect. "When I was a kid, I always wanted to be a damn astronaut. Then Daddy said one day, 'There ain't no black astronauts, you dummy,' and that was that. You know how excited those astronauts must get before they go up into space? This is better.

"And you know what, Tommy? You know why I'm euphoric instead of sad right now? I'm going to be with my sweet Angie again, for the first time since they put me behind bars. She died when I was in, and I've been a prisoner in this life since I got out, because I have to live in a world without her. I'm going to finally be free,

Tommy. Free of all of the struggle and hate in this world."

With the last of his words, they pulled up outside Moses' apartment. Lukas and a few of the Black Eagles were loitering on the stoop or sitting on their bikes. Moses exited the car sloppily. He fished in his pocket and pulled out a key, tossing it to Tommy. "Take this and use it next time you stop by, before you break my damn window."

Tommy called out to the young men, "Take care of him, he's had a rough day and a few too many tonight. Get him up and get him to bed. Mos—I'll see you tomorrow sometime. I love you, man."

Two of the Eagles took Moses under the arms and helped him up the steps to the entrance.

Tommy watched, then pulled away and headed home. Despite the sadness of the drive, he felt good about removing Moses from the plan. *Now it's time to get ready to take care of business.*

18 CHAOS

TOMMY ENTERED HIS DARKENED HOME, full of regret and with all the stealth his career had taught him. He avoided every creaky floorboard and stair on the way to his bedroom. His body was tired, but his mind was clear and wide awake.

His eyes had adjusted to the darkness, and he looked down on his sleeping wife. She wasn't in her normal spot—a safe distance away from his side, across the moat that always separated them.

Now she slept on his side, on his pillow. Her graying hair was tousled, and her mouth was agape. She breathed with a thin rattle and an occasional slight gasp. Even as she slept, she wore her mask of worry.

In the dim light, he could almost smooth out the deep lines in her face and see the fun-loving, vibrant woman he'd married so long ago, before her life as a cop's wife eroded it all. *I never betrayed you, Margie. I never did the things the other guys did. That much, I'm proud of. But you betrayed me, and I never suspected. Some cop I was. No wonder I never made detective.*

He wanted to wake her and tell her. He'd never told her that he never cheated. *She probably assumed I was like the others, and kept herself in denial like their wives all did, for the kids.*

Her hands were folded on top of her abdomen as if she were lying in state, but her rings were askew. He thought about the night of their honeymoon, and how he'd lain there watching her in her beauty and wondering what he had done to get so lucky. He reached over and straightened her rings, and she stirred but didn't wake. *She sleeps well when she's on the sauce.*

He went down the hall and entered Bobby's room. It was moonlit, and the trophies on the dresser were all covered with a thin layer of dust. Toy figurines stood in frozen poses—knights, sorcerers, an astronaut, and several superheroes. The bookshelf held racks of neatly arranged comics. An old magic set sat in its neglected box. *He never did say where he got that. I accused him of stealing it.* Ribbons hung in a jumble on their pegs, sad and neglected. Most of them said the same thing: 'Participant.' *Man, if I'd had his size when I was his age, I could've gone pro. His size with my heart and tenacity, now that would be something.*

The artifacts in the room seemed to cover his son's entire childhood, the things that most grown men would've boxed up by now. *Most men are out of the house by thirty-five, too.*

He thought about the one brief girlfriend Bobby had, and the boy's acute sensitivity. A voice in him, a small voice that wanted to be part of the new kinder, gentler Tommy Borata, spoke to him a little louder this time. *Reach out. Love your son unconditionally, the way he's loved you.* He moved quietly through the door, closing it behind him.

He walked down the darkened hallway and descended the stairs, again taking care not to step on the ones that creaked. *Know your environment.* He made a mental note to repair them over the weekend. *Funny; I might be dead by then, or in the clink.* He thought maybe the boy would fix them if he left a note. *Even funnier.*

He moved into his office and sat at the desk. The clock from the desk set he'd been given on his twentieth anniversary with the force showed the time. *Almost midnight. In twenty-four hours it'll be over. I wish I could sleep.*

He scanned the mementos of his career that lined the walls. Commendations, certificates, photo-ops. Paulie was in most of the pictures, rendering the accomplishments meaningless. *I couldn't save you. I wasn't good enough to save you. My guard was down. Some cop I was. Maybe if someone, some terminally ill hero, had taken out that bastard that shot you earlier, you'd still be around. We might be drinking a few beers, reminiscing on some fishing trip.*

He checked himself in light of his wife's recent revelation. *Not if I'd found out about you and Margie though, you bastard. At least then I could've kicked your ass for that. Some friend;*

you only used me to be close to Margie. Fuck you, pal.

He looked at the few mementos from his four years in the Marine Corps. *They taught me discipline and toughness. I was a warrior.* He picked up a piece of paper from his desk and tacked it to the wall. It was a crayon drawing of a cop with a gun drawn, and a robber on the ground with Xs in his eyes. *I always wanted to be a hero.*

He sat at his desk and went over the plan again in his head. That was the agreement with Moses—nothing would be written down. *No evidence.* It all had to be perfect. He'd summoned all he'd learned in his years on the street and as a cop to come up with it, and he trusted his new friend and partner with his life. Now he would have to go it alone. He didn't care about himself—he really didn't have much to lose or live for at this point. *I wasn't a good father. I wasn't a good husband. It will silence the demons.*

He opened his gun case and inspected each weapon carefully. Each of the handguns was immaculately clean, loaded with an extended clip of hollow-point rounds, racked and ready with the safety on. One by one, they went back into the case. *Tucking the kids back into bed. Tomorrow will be a long day.*

He left the office and entered the darkened kitchen. Opening the refrigerator, he took a long, cold slug from the container of milk on the top shelf. After replacing it, he shut the refrigerator door, then reached up and opened the rarely used cabinet well above and behind it. It was high enough that he couldn't see inside, but he moved his hand around like a blind tarantula until he found the bottle he knew was there and pulled it down. It was almost empty. *She's been busy with this stuff.*

He opened the top and smelled the scotch inside. The scent was heavenly and filled him immediately with desire to consume it. The wave of electricity through his body was not unlike sexual arousal, and his heart, mind, and physical being all urged him to tip it up and empty it into himself. *Go for it—what does it matter now? Might as well enjoy it one more time. What the hell, she does.*

He held the bottle up toward the window. The light from the full moon illuminated the amber contents and made it glow like liquid gold. It called to him. *You're a stupid fucking drunk. You stayed in the patrol car so you could have the last of that flask while Paulie went in for your lunch and died. You were drunk and slow, and Paulie died.*

His gaze caught the rows of pill bottles on the counter—some his, some hers, even some for the kid. They called to him as well. *Why not? Because you have a job to do.*

He opened his and took the prescribed amounts of each, washing them down with a handful of tap water. He picked up Margie's pill containers one by one until he found the one labeled Xanax, opened it and removed two of the pills.

He went to the living room next and eased into the recliner. He placed the bottle of booze and the pills on the stand next to it. Without having to look, he placed his hand on the remote control and hit the power button. The local channel had a classic movie running. He leaned all the way back, almost horizontal, and the chair seemed to cradle and consume him. He reached his arms back and interlaced his fingers behind his head, finally letting himself relax. His mind continued to wander, tired but restless.

~*~

The priest didn't enjoy the rigorous routine but found the anticipation that built through each step of it arousing. He moved through his small, darkened quarters, stepping around his packed suitcases to close window shades and check that the doors were locked. When he was satisfied, he entered the small study and seated himself at his desk. He disconnected his laptop's Ethernet cable and wireless connection, and then turned it on, booting into safe mode as an extra measure of precaution. *Time to relax for a bit before heading to the airport.*

After the boot was complete, he opened a command shell and typed the instructions to mount an encrypted drive from its hidden partition. He entered the password carefully, as it was set to wipe the drive clean on a single bad attempt.

As he waited, he spun in his chair and double-checked that the room was properly blacked out. He turned back to the computer and opened the false calculator app, entering the proper numeric sequence to unlock the entryway to his final destination: his cherished gallery of pictures.

The secrecy and waiting had fully stimulated him, and he began to massage himself through his pants with one hand, while his other deftly controlled the mouse, flipping through the photos of his prizes.

Oh yes, this one. Such a sweet little boy. My little cherub...

Ah, Danny. So feisty. Such a difficult conquest. I so much enjoyed the challenging ones...

Little orphan Lucy, not quite my cup of tea, but variety is the spice of life, they say...

As his level of stimulation came close to its peak, he rose from the chair and moved to his small bedroom. After removing his clothing, he lay on the bed, reached over and squirted lotion onto his hand from a small container on the nightstand.

He serviced himself but struggled to get back to the pinnacle. He found his mind drifting from the laptop images to the confrontation earlier in the day. His frustration mounted as he tried to focus on the more pleasurable of the two, but was unable. He removed his hand from his now-limp dick and wiped himself clean with the bedspread as his excitement slid to anger.

He frustration mounted, and he muttered to himself, lying on the bed. "Fucking cop. We mustn't get angry. Bad things happen when we get angry. We make mistakes."

"You already made mistakes."

The priest jerked his head from the pillow and attempted to jump to his feet. "You!" he shouted. As he reached a half-sitting position, he saw sparks and then long silvery threads flying through the air toward him.

His next sensation was complete rigidity, his body turned to stone. *Like Lot's wife*, he thought briefly in his confusion. He was cognizant but incapacitated physically. He fought for control, but as fifty thousand volts pulsed rhythmically through his body, he fell back onto the bed helplessly and felt his bowels release.

When it stopped, he again attempted to rise, but his body only jerked and spasmed in response. He tried to keep his eyes on his attacker, but they wouldn't focus, and the lack of light obscured him. Suddenly, the darkness exploded into a burst of brilliant white stars as he felt a blow to his head and lost consciousness.

He came to slowly and tried to regain his bearings. His head was splitting, and his mouth was gagged. He was bound at the hands and feet, lying on the bed, and his entire body ached. His eyes focused past the bedroom and out into the study. He saw a figure seated at his desk, methodically deleting his gallery of pictures.

The beginnings of a shout were suppressed as he thought better of it, and he strained to think, to find a solution. *We always wriggle out of everything.*

The intruder rose from the desk and came toward him. He feigned sleep, hoping to catch the attacker off-guard and gain the upper hand.

"This is for my old man."

It was the last thing he heard before another blow took him back into unconsciousness.

He woke briefly, his head banging off objects as he was dragged across the building by his feet.

He came to again, this time finding himself prone on a cold, hard surface. He realized he was still naked. His eyes adjusted to the brilliant light above him, and he squinted. Through a halo of gold, he saw the beaten, dead face of Jesus on the massive cross above, looking down on him. The stained-glass windows on the periphery of his blurred vision swirled like kaleidoscopes. *I'm on the altar. Why am I on the altar?* He looked down the length of his body to see that he'd been duct-taped to the slab at his chest, waist, and feet.

His question was answered, to his horror, as he saw the intruder approach with a large knife.

"No," he screamed through the gag. "No, no, no."

"Vengeance is mine, and recompense, for the time when their foot shall slip; for the day of their calamity is at hand, and their doom comes swiftly," the intruder spoke as he neared.

The priest knew the attacker's intent, and so he closed his eyes and clenched his teeth to prepare himself. He tried to block all sensation with his mind, but nothing could beat back the searing, sharp pain as the tool of his offenses was hacked from him. His groin throbbed, and he felt the warm rush of blood as it poured out of him and around his lower body.

From there he felt no pain, as his body went into shock and his life began to slip away. The last things his senses brought to him were the sound of liquid being poured out, the nauseating smell of gasoline, the flare of a match, the beauty of a shroud of multi-hued red and orange flames surrounding him, and finally the burning of his own wicked flesh.

Forgive me, Father, for I have sinned. Take me, and do what you please…

~*~

Tommy became aware of sunlight beginning to make its way into the room and the morning local newscast droning on through its usual litany: sports, weather, financial, war, death, hatred, politics. He had one foot in the present and one in the fragmented jumble of dreams when he first heard the ominous 'breaking news' music. He paid it no mind and started to drift again until he began to pick up the pieces subconsciously.

"…SWAT teams engaged…"

In his dream, he was sitting on the bank of the pond, fishing with Bobby. Margie was next to them on a spread-out blanket, unpacking their lunch from a wicker picnic basket.

"…church…"

He looked across the pond and saw a priest walking along a path. The priest stopped and stared back, then made the sign of the cross at them and continued on his way. He was whistling, and his gait was carefree.

"...engulfed in fire..."

As they sat peacefully, Moses approached without a word and sat beside them. Margie greeted him with a kiss and handed him an ice-cold beer from the cooler.

"...castration..."

Bobby yelled that he had one on the line, a big one. He yanked back the rod and wound the reel to bring it in. Tommy asked if he needed help, but he refused. Moses urged him to bring it in, and Margie clapped her hands and danced with glee on the shoreline.

"...Father Damien Tarat..."

Bobby continued to tug and reel until his catch bobbed to the surface and made its way toward them, a wake spreading behind the body of a priest at the end of his line.

Tommy shook off the lingering effects of deep sleep and rocketed up out of the recliner, shouting "Jesus!" He stood swaying and half-awake in front of the television.

A reporter was standing in front of a burning church, bathed, along with the scene, in swirling, flashing red and blue lights. The colored lights danced off the shattered stained glass, and yellow tape encircled the building. Tommy stood transfixed. His repeated shouts of "No!" filled the air around him, but sounded as if they must've been coming from someone else.

The reporter continued excitedly, "Again, the word we have here is that a lone attacker entered the church rectory late last night, subdued Father Tarat and took him into the main area of the church. Area 911 services reported receiving an emergency call from the building, with the caller repeating the following biblical verses:

'Rescue the weak and needy; Deliver them out of the hand of the wicked. Since indeed God considers it just to repay with affliction those who afflict you. O Lord, God of vengeance, O God of vengeance, shine forth! Vengeance is mine, and recompense, for the time when their foot shall slip; for the day of their calamity is at hand, and their doom comes swiftly.'

"Police responded, and the man emerged from the church with a gun. Police had no choice other than to fire on him. After firefighters doused the blaze, they found the remains of Father Tarat laid out on the altar. Police are working to identify the assailant. Father Tarat had been accused of molesting altar boys and several other children."

"Oh my God, what happened? I heard you yelling. What happened at the church?" It was Margie, standing next to him in her robe. "I'm so glad you're home, Tommy," she said, hugging him. "Who did this?" she asked.

"Uh...I don't know. They didn't say yet. Probably one of his victims..." His mind tried to process, but stalled, mired down with shock. Pieces clicked slowly together as if pulled by magnets through water.

He disengaged from Margie and ran up the stairs. *I don't remember if he was even in there sleeping, I just assumed...* He checked Bobby's room, then hurtled back down the stairs and out the door.

19 DISCOVERIES

HIS MIND RACING NOW along with his vehicle, Tommy pulled up in front of Moses' apartment and jumped out of the car, reaching into his pocket for the key. He ran up the stairs and burst through the door, scanning the room.

The kitchen table held a coffee cup, a pen, and several sheets of blank paper. He was careful not to touch anything. His former colleagues would figure it out soon, and be by to shut the place down.

The shock of it was still washing over him in waves. He looked to the bathroom and thought of Moses being sick in there. He looked to the couch and the old TV and thought of Moses. He looked to the stash box and thought of Moses.

Footsteps came up the stairs, and he turned to find Lukas coming through the door with an envelope.

"Hey. Uncle Mos said you'd be by. Said to give this to you. Only you."

He's doesn't know. Tommy took it from his outstretched hand. "Thanks," he said, as Lukas disappeared down the stairs. Tommy wondered if he should've told him right then and there, but decided to read the note first.

My brother Tommy,

Time was getting short for me, I hope you understand. I had to do what I did, for all the reasons we discussed, and more. I came home last night and sat at this table thinking about the mistreatment by evil people of good souls like your son and entire races of people, and became very angry. I had to do it before I sobered up too much. You know how that hard stuff affects me.

Anyway, I couldn't have you back out of this on my account or cut me out. You still have hope, and a lot to live for, and I was at the end of the line. What needed to be done is done. I was tired of being sick, and the government won't let us die with dignity. I didn't want to suffer any longer.

I hope this buys me some retribution, and hopefully, as you read this, I'm back with my sweet Angie, in Elysium. I'm cancer-free, I suffer no more, and now I know all the answers. Hopefully, we're all the same color where I am, or at least not judgmental about such a silly thing. I wonder if once the flesh is gone, all of the evil we perpetrate upon each other in lust of it will be gone as well.

Carry forward, my friend, take care of your wife. Talk to your boy, love your son, and keep me in your thoughts. I love you, man.

Moses Taylor, astronaut, husband of Angie the Angel, friend of Tommy, Vigilante Angel.

He sat on the couch and re-read it a few times, then folded the note and descended the stairs to talk to Lukas, to break the news as he'd had to so many times before, on the job. He reached the bottom and was about to turn the corner to the first-floor apartments when he saw Lukas sitting alone on the stoop outside.

"Hey, kid," Tommy said as he sat beside the youth.

"Save it. I just found out. Word gets around quick in the 'hood."

Tommy knew to remain silent.

"Uncle fucking Mos, going all fucking Rambo and shit. Damn. Is this your motherfucking shit, white man? You get him all worked up and into this vigilante shit? You all always up there plotting about some bullshit. You use him to do your dirt?"

Now he had to respond. "No. I'm pissed off at him, and I'm all fucked up about this. He went off on his own. He was sick, Lukas. Damn sick. He wanted to make a difference, I guess. He kept talking about trying to do something to make up for the wrong he did a long time ago. I told him he already paid for that."

Lukas considered his words a moment. "But you were into some shit like that. You were planning something?"

"It's better not to talk about it, Lukas. You know how that goes. Your uncle and me were both real sick. That puts a man into a different mindset, gives him a tremendous amount of power.

"We both had a lot to make up for, and yeah, we talked about that. But I never wanted him to do something like this alone. He was sick of being sick, and he hated that fucking priest for hurting kids, like I did. He hurt my fucking kid, and I think that's one of the things that motivated Mos. He stole my thunder there, and I'm a little angry about it. The cops'll be here soon; I have to go."

Lukas was sniffing, fighting back tears. "I know he loved you, cracker. He talked about your white ass all the time. Never thought I'd see the day some damn white cop come waltzing in here without getting an ass-beating."

"Yeah. I loved him too. I'll be in touch. Let's give him a good send-off. I'll help out; keep me in the loop on the arrangements. You'll find my number in your uncle's address book. I got to roll, Lukas. Cops are going to be all over this place soon. Go upstairs and clean house, don't say too much."

"I hear you. That's one thing we're damn good at."

Tommy left the building and paused, hoping to hear the scrape of the window opening high above. He turned and looked up, half-expecting, half-wishing to see Moses' head emerge through it.

He wiped his eyes with his sleeve and walked toward his car.

~*~

The afternoon sun pierced Tommy's closed eyelids, waking him. He could hear the drone of the newscast before his eyes could adjust to the light. He leaned away from the window and rose up slightly from the living room couch to find Bobby sitting in the recliner next to him.

"Day off?" he asked Bobby.

"Night shift."

"Where's your mother?"

"Aunt Diane's."

They watched the coverage in silence. Sadness, paranoia, and fear continued their assault on Tommy. The excited reporter was standing in front of the cordoned-off church again, rattling off the details as the screen filled with a dated picture of Moses.

"...we've just received word the deceased assailant has been identified as Moses Taylor. His motive is currently unknown..."

"Dad...that's your friend..." Bobby said.

Tommy grabbed the remote to increase the volume.

"We'll be back with more details as we find them out. This is Jenna March, News 12. John, back to you in the studio."

Tommy turned off the TV but continued looking at it.

"You okay, Dad? You've got a weird look on your face. Did you know he was going to do this? Did he say anything to you?"

"No, son. I mean—we saw all this in the news when we were getting treatment. It upset us both. We said some things, sure. I bet a lot of people did, right? There can't be much doubt the priest did it—all those lives he ruined, those kids."

This time it was Bobby who offered an awkward silence and uncomfortable posture.

"Bobby, Moses said something to me. That I should talk to you. It was after we all worked together back on Thanksgiving," Tommy said.

Bobby hesitated, considering whether to finally confront what they'd remained silent about for years. "Yeah, we took a break and went outside for a while and talked. He brought up the priest then."

"What did he say?" Tommy asked, anxious to keep the conversation going. He was scared of what Moses might've told his son, and terrified of what his son might be about to tell him.

"Actually, it was me who did most of the talking. I told him about it. What happened a long time ago."

"Listen, Bobby—we don't need to..."

Bobby's voice rose in anger. "Yes. Yes, Dad. We do need to. We've always needed to. Some things are too painful to keep inside for so long. You need to hear it, and you need to deal with things. We all do. We can't live in denial. We can't fix what we're afraid to confront."

Tommy slumped back in acceptance. He thought of Moses by his side, and it gave him courage. "Okay, it's okay. I love you, son. Go ahead."

"That priest got me too, Dad. I talked to Moses about it. I had to talk to someone, and

Moses was easy to talk to. He had some bad things happen to him too when he was a kid; maybe that's why he did what he did."

Bobby paused, not noticing the tears flowing down the face of his tough, hardened father. "Why do you think I was always ducking church?"

"Why? Why not tell me and your mother?"

"I didn't think you wanted to hear it. He threatened me. I was a kid, and I was scared and embarrassed. So many reasons, Dad. But it's over now. We have to move on together."

Tommy flinched at the words. "Ah, Jesus, Bobby. I'm so damn proud of you. C'mere kid."

Bobby moved over to the couch, beside his father. Tommy put his arm around him and held him tight, still crying. "I'm so sorry, son. I'm so fucking sorry. I wasn't there for you," he sobbed, his tears falling onto his son's neck.

Bobby pulled away and looked his father in the eye. "While we're at it, there's something else, Dad. Another elephant we have to get out of the room. Or the closet."

Despite Bobby's attempt to inject some humor into the subject, Tommy looked at the floor, more out of shame than the awkwardness of the moment. He saved his son the trouble of the revelation.

"Yeah, I know. I guess I always have and didn't want to admit it. I was always this hard-ass, so afraid of facing my friends that I gave my son a miserable life."

"It wasn't, Dad. We all live with our secrets. You made me a better man in a lot of ways. We've had a good life, a good family."

"I didn't protect you from that son of a bitch. I'm supposed to protect people, and I didn't protect my own son. Maybe if I had…"

"Dad, it wasn't because of him that I'm gay. I've always been that way. C'mon. You know it. In the beginning, I tried to be this sports-playing, outdoorsy kid to please you, but it wasn't me. Maybe that's why he targeted me. After what happened, I didn't care anymore. Doesn't matter. He's gone. We have to move forward—you, me, and Mom."

"Yeah, we do. I love you, son. Unconditionally."

They both turned as Margie entered the room. "Tommy, I'm so sorry about Moses…"

Tommy went to her and embraced her. It was the first time he could remember her going to her sister's and not coming home smelling like booze. He wondered if they had a chance.

"He was a good man. He taught me a lot. The last thing he did was to remind me how lucky I am, and how special and important you two are. I'm so sorry for the way I've been acting. I love you, honey. Let's have breakfast. We have a lot to talk about, our little family."

20 THE VISITATION

TOMMY AND HIS FAMILY made their way through the media outside and entered the funeral parlor's stuffy viewing room. They walked past the sparse groups in the sea of padded folding chairs, toward the casket ahead, where his friend Moses lay.

He took note of the few floral arrangements and looked for theirs. The sweet smell and choral music flowing through the room's speakers began to nauseate him.

"You go," Margie said as they reached the front.

Tommy knelt at the altar of his friend and looked down on his tortured body. There were mementos in the casket—folded, handwritten notes, a few small pictures, and a New York

Rangers cap. Tommy reached out and touched the waxen hands, folded together to hold rosary beads, and spoke softly as his tears began to flow.

"I'm sorry, Mos. I'm so sorry. I never should've gotten you mixed up in this crazy scheme. I should've gone it alone. You were my best friend, and you died because of me, like Paulie. You made me better, brother. I'll never forget you."

He reached into his jacket pocket, withdrew a small astronaut figurine, and placed it alongside his friend. He said a half-hearted prayer—for Moses' sake more than out of any hope it would make a difference—wiped his face with a handkerchief from his breast pocket, and stood. He looked Moses over again and moved aside to let Margie and Bobby have their turn. He walked up the aisle to accusatory stares from Moses' silent family members and friends.

He chose a seat in the back of the room, and his family joined him after paying their respects. Someone squeezed his shoulder, and he turned to see Carmen and Beulah walk past, down the aisle. They nodded in his direction.

He watched as they stood over Moses and then knelt together. They both touched him lovingly and said their prayers with sincerity. They rose and walked up the aisle, sitting in the row in front of Tommy and his family. Tommy rose to kiss them on the cheek and whisper introductions to his family.

"I'm so sorry, Tommy," Carmen said.

"Yeah," was all he could manage, fighting back tears.

"Your husband is a good man," she said to Margie. "And he talks about you all the time," she added to Bobby.

"That's a shocker," Bobby replied.

"How you feeling, Tommy?" Beulah asked.

"Not so well. I'm a wreck, especially with all of this. I miss him. I need him."

She reached back and squeezed his hand. "We miss you, Tommy. Stop in and say hello to everyone sometime."

"Yeah, I will," he lied.

Eddie Silver and his son Saul entered and made their way down the row to sit next to Tommy. "Hey, how you doing?" Eddie asked.

"I'm good, Eddie." The man looked twenty years older, the chemo having ravaged him since they last met.

Saul unfolded a paper and showed it to Tommy. "I drawed this, for Mr. Moses."

Tommy took the page. It was a crayon drawing of a black superhero, in full cape and with an 'M' emblazoned on its chest. Beneath it, in childish scrawl, it said "Moses Tayler, Super Hero."

"It's beautiful, kid," Tommy said as he folded it and handed it back, trying not to cry.

Eddie leaned over to whisper into Tommy's ear. "I hear the cops are all over this, trying to figure out if it was some kind of conspiracy or whatever. Just doesn't seem to add up. We're going up to see Moses. We'll be right back."

He watched as the father and son knelt before Moses and paid their respects, large and small yarmulkes on their heads. He thought back with regret about his first interaction with the sick man. The boy placed his drawing beside Moses.

As they retook their seats next to him, Tommy heard a droning sound outside and knew what would come next. Within a few minutes, Lukas and the rest of the Black Eagles entered the church. Their black leather vests and bright patches stood out in the drab room. Lukas nodded in Tommy's direction before greeting and consoling the members of his family.

The pastor entered and conducted a solemn service over the sounds of sniffling and crying. Tommy shifted in his seat and then excused himself. He found the restroom in the main hall connecting the visitation rooms and hurried through the door in time to kneel before the toilet and empty the contents of his stomach in a series of heaves. While fighting to breathe, he thought of Moses getting sick in his bathroom not long ago.

As he was cleaning himself up, the door opened behind him, and he saw Lukas in the mirror. "Damn, white boy. This shit reeks in here. You okay?"

"Not really. Got a bug or something, I guess."

Lukas stood at the urinal and relieved himself. "Listen. I sort of know what you two crazy bastards were doing. I know my uncle had a lot of regrets and wanted some kind of absolution."

"You use a lot of big words for a biker guy."

"What are you saying?" Lukas asked angrily.

"Never mind. Forget it."

"Anyway, I think I'm putting this all together, what you two were up to. I ain't saying shit to nobody. But I get it. You plan anything else, let me know if I can help. Uncle Mos would want that. We got your back. That's all I'm saying. I'm down with the concept."

Tommy's paranoia grew, with the second hint in less than an hour that others might be putting things together. He nodded but didn't respond, and left the bathroom.

Disappointed the nausea hadn't stopped, Tommy walked back into the room as the pastor was asking if anyone had anything to say for Moses. The occupants of the room all turned to look at him, and he froze. After a brief, awkward pause, they realized he wasn't there to do so, and turned back to the pastor, who finished the service.

As he and his group rose to leave, Lukas walked up to them.

"We're going to have some food over at the diner up the road. Got a private room, just some sandwiches, and what-not. You're all welcome to stop by."

"Thanks," Tommy said for the group, without committing. He wanted to get home to his couch and pretend none of this nightmare ever happened.

21 THE SUSPECT

TOMMY FIDGETED in the ancient wooden swivel chair and looked across the desk at the man seated behind it. He and Roger, who was now Chief of Detectives Patterson, had come up through the force together. Tommy waited, picking at the ripped vinyl on the chair while Patterson leafed through a folder.

Outside the office, he watched the usual buzz of cops coming in from their shifts, and those just getting to work and preparing to go out. He noticed familiar faces, and they all seemed to glance his way—the cop who'd encountered him parked outside of Murphy's, the cop who'd responded to the ruckus at Wyla's, Davis, the undercover cop who'd watched the door while they roughed up Buster Vela, and the cop who'd stopped them outside the church rectory. He started to wonder if it was all coincidence that they were coming and going as he sat in the office with Patterson, and he started to sweat and regret everything he'd become involved in. *I couldn't just be smart, retire quietly and fight this damn disease?*

Patterson tossed the folder on the desk, and it slid toward Tommy. Tommy reached for it, and the chief shook his head. "No. C'mon, Borata. You know better." The chief pulled the folder back toward him.

"Listen, Tommy. Seems straightforward enough to me. Taylor had a note on him. Said that someone close to him was a victim, and he wanted revenge since he was dying anyway. If it's up to me, case closed."

"Makes sense to me," Tommy said, beginning to rise.

"Not so fast," the chief said. Tommy plopped back down. "See that guy over there?" He gestured through the glass front of his office and out into the station-house floor area.

Tommy saw a tall, burly cop with a flat-top and crisp uniform. *Looks like me, a long time ago. Ambitious. Tough.* The man turned and looked at Tommy casually, as if he'd sensed Tommy's eyes on him. *Good intuition.*

The chief interrupted Tommy's inspection. "That's Carson. Used to be an Olympic boxer. He came in as a transfer last year. He just made detective, and he's ambitious; angling to take over for me when I retire. A real up-and-comer, everything by the book, no stone unturned. He's been asking around about this. The talk around the station that you and Taylor were buddies has reached him, so he's been asking about you."

"Well, thanks for sticking up for me," Tommy said. "I'm sure they have a lot more to do around here than worry about some conspiracy theory about a broke-down old cop with cancer."

Patterson rose. "Well, either way, Borata, keep a low profile and stay the hell out of trouble. Say hello to Margie and the boy."

As Tommy got up to shake his hand, a wave of nausea and pain hit him. He covered it to get out of there as quickly as possible. He left the chief's office and headed down the hall toward the exit. His discomfort got worse with every step, and he eyed his goal, the red 'Exit' sign at the end of the hall. With every office door and cubicle he passed, he expected Carson to pop out and confront him.

By the time he was halfway there, he was leaning against the wall for support. A few steps later he felt close to passing out. He reached the door to the men's room and ducked inside.

He went to the handicapped stall, as he always had when he'd worked there, for its extra space. He plopped down on the toilet to regain his composure, pressed with his fingers at the source of the pain, under his right rib cage, and he knew. *Fuck. Liver. It's back, and it's spreading.* He fussed with the toilet paper dispenser, his old nemesis. Finally, he found the end of the roll and yanked a long trail out to mop his sweat-drenched head.

Someone entered, and he listened, waiting for the sound of piss against porcelain to stop. He fought the sharp pain in his abdomen enough to lean down to see the intruder's shoes. *Spit-shine. Must be that motherfucker.* He waited while the sink ran, and then through an interminable washing and blow-drying of hands. *Just dry them on your pants like everyone else, dick-head. This guy is patient.*

And then there was silence. He waited for the sound of the other man leaving. Nothing. Minutes passed. He pulled more toilet paper and then flushed the toilet for effect. The water drained, and the toilet refilled, and he still hadn't heard the door open and close. He peeked again and saw the shoes.

Finally, the door squeaked open and then slowly closed. He struggled to his feet. As he exited the stall, he saw the younger mirror image of himself leaning against the closed door.

"Borata. You fell for the old fake door-closing trick. You're losing your touch," Carson said.

"It's Tommy. Call me Tommy. Listen, I'm in some pain…"

He moved toward the door, but Carson didn't budge.

"I never saw someone take a crap without dropping trou," Carson said.

Tommy's anger surpassed his fear of the man. "I'm sick. I ducked in here to puke and get a fucking break for a minute. It's embarrassing, okay? What can I do for you, Carson?"

"I'm going to be the new chief of detectives here. I know all about you, Borata. You have quite a reputation. And, apparently, a lot of friends here on the force. I'm still checking this whole thing with the priest's murder and might have some questions. Maybe you can shed some light on that nigger Taylor, and his motive…"

The pain left Tommy for a moment, as adrenaline surged and he pinned the man to the door with one strong hand around his throat.

Carson smiled, in denial of his discomfort and inability to breathe.

Tommy let go. "He was my friend, and a far better man than you, I'd bet. Do what you want with me, but don't ever use that fucking word again, or say a bad thing about that man."

Carson stepped aside, and Tommy took his opportunity to leave. As he did, Carson said, "Don't leave town, as they say. And get well soon."

"There ain't no getting well from this, asshole. Pray you never have to know firsthand. In fact, I hope you do someday."

22 CONCLUSION

HE PAUSED AT THE ENTRANCE to the unit. It was all the same, with one glaring exception. His pod was empty, but strangers sat in Moses' seat and the others. He'd just started into the room when he felt a hand on his arm.

"Hey, stranger. How're you feeling?" It was Carmen.

"Been better. Can't say I'm happy to be back here, other than to see you and Beulah."

"Let's get you fixed up and out of here." She helped him over and began his saline drip. "We'll get you juiced up while we wait for your cocktail to arrive."

He tried to smile, but the weight of being there, without Moses, was too much. Beulah yelled an enthusiastic greeting to him from across the unit, and he offered her a lighthearted wave in response.

"How's the gang, any of them still coming around?" he asked.

She was hesitant. "Well, Helen is with Moses now. You saw Eddie at the funeral. He's in hospice. He didn't want to continue treatment, doc said it wouldn't do much good."

He surveyed the others in his section while she worked on him. They seemed to him like inanimate, doomed vessels. He glared at the sleeping man in Moses' seat. *Asshole.* He couldn't pull himself away from his anger and sadness.

What the fuck am I doing here?

"C'mon, Tommy," she said. He thought he'd said it to himself, but apparently, his lips had betrayed him. *My whole body is betraying me.* She took him by the chin and lifted his head up to look her in her eyes. "I need you to suck it up, Chief."

"Yeah, I'll be okay. Just a brief pity party and I'll be good to go, Nurse Ratched."

She laughed at the reference, still looking into his eyes, and it brought a smile to his face as well.

He flipped on his pod's TV. It was the news channel, again. He ignored the temptation to shut it down. He leaned back and closed his eyes, thinking about Moses. They had achieved their goal; they'd made the world a slightly better place, but he'd lost his friend. His feelings ran an endless loop between sad, conflicted, guilty, empty, and unfulfilled.

I thought my wife and I were devoted to each other. I thought my son was going to be a man's man. I thought I'd have grandkids and a long retirement. Everything I thought was wrong. I'm under investigation. What the fuck do I have to live for.

He let his mind drift back to the better days and better people in that same unit. He reminisced about his life, the good and the bad, while the newscasters droned on about all of the horrible things humans were busy doing to each other.

"...financial adviser who has swindled his elderly clients..."

"…charity organizer apparently paid himself a high salary and gave little to the cause…"

"…the senator raided funds intended to do meaningful things in his community…"

Carmen came back to check on him. "What do you say, tough guy? We can't beat this damn thing if you aren't on board."

He looked at her and scanned the room again. *Moses isn't here. Moses is dead. Moses is dead. Moses is dead. Dead like Paulie, and once again I did nothing, and I'm alive. Useless.* He saw a man sitting in a pod in the unit on the far side, wired up to an infusion console, a patch over one eye. *Sensei Molletier.*

"I guess I'll try to stick around a while, Carmen," he said.

I have little time left and a lot of work to do. This time his lips didn't give him away.

The End

Preview: Book II: The Cop

Brad Carson enjoyed his image in a full-length locker room mirror, adjusting his holster to the angle he preferred—low on the hip like an old-west gunslinger. Despite making Detective, he often still preferred his crisply pressed black tactical police uniform. He pulled his service semi-automatic from the holster and took a firing stance, aiming for his own forehead, laughing as he replaced it.

"It's a good day to bust some bad hombres. You ready to roll, Jackson?" he asked.

"Locked and loaded. Let's hit the Batmobile. I'm in the mood to crack some skulls. That's said off the record, of course."

The two men left the locker room and walked through the cacophony of the station-house.

"Make way, losers," Carson announced to the room. "Two bad-ass PO-lice officers coming through. Feel free to admire us, but please don't touch. It's okay to take notes, take pictures. *This* is what you should strive to become."

He paused at a female officer's desk, struck a pose, and said "Yeah, I'm busy, but try again another time. I'm very booked up. Maybe I'll squeeze you in, or squeeze into you, if you catch my drift."

The woman lurched from her chair at him as if to attack, but stopped short.

Carson didn't flinch and laughed at her attempt to faze him.

"Fuck you, Carson," she said.

He moved along and stopped at another desk. "Jesus Christ. Bobby Borata, I do believe you get fatter every time I walk past you. Do you have a desk drawer full of Ring-Dings, Bobby?"

A thin wave of laughter wafted through the room, and Carson soaked up the attention. The officer didn't respond, so he tried again. "You've got to shape up, Borata. Square that sloppy uniform away. It looks like you slept in it. Wasn't your old man a Marine? Didn't he teach you anything?"

Bobby looked at him. "Keep my old man out of this, Carson."

"Hard to do, Borata. I'm looking at him hard for this priest murder. Conspiracy and all that. Him and his buddy Moses, who is, shall we say, no longer with us."

"Leave my father alone, Carson," Bobby cautioned again.

"He'll be alone, in the joint, except for when he's getting it in the can from his cellmate."

Bobby came out from behind his desk awkwardly and tried to grab Carson, but was expertly placed in a choke-hold, his head directed down toward Carson's crotch.

"Do me, Bobby!" Carson yelled as he jerked Bobby's head up and down.

The room erupted in laughter, and a door burst open as Chief of Detectives Patterson emerged. "What the fuck is going on here? Knock this shit off and get your asses to work. Carson, let go of him. *Now.*"

Carson released his grip. "You best get back to your martial arts training, Borata. It will never top my cage skills, though. If you want to be a cop, get your ass in shape. Get out from behind that desk once in a while."

Carson and Jackson made their way out of the building to their unmarked car in the parking lot. "You drive, I'll ride shotgun today," Carson said.

Jackson started the engine as they strapped in and prepared to leave. "Where to first?" Jackson asked.

"Head on to the 'hood. Back to the Taylor place. I want to shake that nephew down—see if he'll talk to me. Maybe he's ready to say what he knows about old man Borata's involvement with his uncle offing the priest."

"You want me to plant a bag on him?" Jackson asked. "That'll give you some leverage."

"Yeah, in fact, that might work. I have to get this thing moving if I'm gonna get promoted next cycle."

Jackson slowed down as they drove through the city's blighted section. They both lowered their windows and stared menacingly at the people on the street, who froze in place at the sight of them. Movement and conversations stopped until they had moved past. "I love this shit," Carson said. "I love to intimidate. Call me The Intimidator. That'll be my superhero name."

They pulled up next to a tall, muscular overly-made up woman with a large afro, wearing a short dress standing at a corner. "Hello, honey," Carson greeted her. "Haven't seen you in town before. Got stuck working the early shift today, huh?"

She looked around uncomfortably, as if deciding on a route to escape.

"Don't be nervous," Carson added. "You know your boss, Charlie the pimp? Well, we're kind of *his* boss. So it's all cool. Except we might need some favors occasionally from you, understand?"

She nodded, and they moved on.

"I believe I'll get me some of that black sugar," Carson said.

"You do know that was a dude, right, Carson?" Jackson asked.

"The hell it was," Carson replied. His face reddened with embarrassment. "These street women are rough, that's all."

"Nah, that was a dude. You just hit on a dude. Maybe you have some latent homosexual tendencies there, Carson."

Carson flew into a rage. "Shut the fuck up, Jackson. Of course I knew it. I was just fucking around, you understand? Nothing less. Don't think about embarrassing me about any shit like that around the station, you understand?"

"Alright, alright. Calm down. Jesus."

Carson continued to fume as they approached a bodega. A very large man was leaning against the building, smoking a cigarette. "Hold up, Jackson," Carson said.

They stopped, and Carson got out of the car and approached the man. "What's up, brother-man? You causing trouble?" he asked.

The man looked at him uneasily. "I'm not doing anything wrong. Not holding, not soliciting. Just got off my shift. Graveyard."

"You're loitering though, right? Stay where you are," Carson ordered. He opened the door to the store and summoned the clerk. The Asian woman came outside.

"Didn't you call in about some guy shoplifting?" Carson asked her.

"Wait a minute, what is this?" the man objected.

"Shut up, or you're going down," Carson responded sharply.

The clerk wore a confused expression, appearing to wonder if she heard him correctly. "No. Nobody cause trouble today. Quiet day so far."

"Go back inside," Carson ordered her.

Jackson got out of the vehicle and walked over. "Is this man resisting arrest, Detective Carson?" he asked.

"He might be in a minute. Let's see." Carson grabbed the man and spun him, pushing him up against the wall.

"Come on, man," the man complained.

Carson kicked his legs apart and yanked his hands behind him, cuffing them tightly. He jammed his elbow into the center of the man's back and pushed his face into the wall. "Hold still," he shouted. Carson turned to enjoy the attention from the passing traffic as cars slowed to watch what was happening. He patted the man down, yanking bills, change, cigarettes, and a lighter out and onto the sidewalk.

Jackson picked up the pack of cigarettes and ripped the top open, dumping them onto the street. He examined them to see if any were joints. "All clear," he said.

Carson removed the cuffs and spun the man back around. His face was bleeding, and he wore an angry expression.

"Police brutality. You should be ashamed of yourselves," the man said.

Carson laughed as they got back into their car. "Have a nice day, buddy. Stay outta trouble." He bent and picked up a few of the larger bills. "And thanks for the tip." As they pulled away, he watched as the man bent to pick up his belongings. "I love this job. What else is a bully gonna do after high school, when you can't kick ass anymore?"

"We're just keeping the streets safe for the citizens, in our own special way," Jackson added. "You know, too bad he was clean. The more of them we put into cages, the cleaner and safer my city becomes."

"We need a bigger zoo," Carson laughed. "There they are, just up ahead, dancing in the street like a bunch of goddamn monkeys. Hold up here and let's observe for a few minutes. Maybe they'll fire up a joint. Then park as close to those bikes as you can, block them in. Call our location in to the station while we wait."

f you enjoyed this book, please leave a brief review at your favorite book site. Thanks!

Sign up for the newsletter at billydecarlo.com to stay informed about progress and release dates for new books, audiobooks, and other news.

Other books by Billy DeCarlo

Billy DeCarlo

Billy DeCarlo is an American author of novels and short stories.

A Note to My Readers

At my core, I'm just a humble, blue-collar guy who has always loved to write. To be honest, I don't seek fame; perhaps just enough fortune to pay the bills. I write because I need to write.

The most rewarding thing a writer can receive is a review from those who enjoyed the work.

The most constructive thing a writer can receive is a private message with anything that can help to improve his or her work.

I do hope that you sign up for the newsletter at my website so that you hear about future books, editions, and other news.

Reviews are the currency of the craft. If you enjoyed my book, please take time to write a review. Thank you and I hope you enjoyed this book!

billydecarlo.com

facebook.com/BillyDeCarloAuthor

twitter.com/BillyDeCarlo1

patreon.com/billydecarlo

goodreads.com/author/show/16887417.Billy_DeCarlo

https://www.amazon.com/Billy-DeCarlo/e/B06XJZF8Z3

Made in the USA
Middletown, DE
25 June 2022